Par for the Course

Par for the Course

A Novel

RAY BLACKSTON

New York   Boston   Nashville

FaithWords
Hachette Book Group USA
237 Park Avenue
New York, NY 10017

Visit our Web site at www.faithwords.com.

Printed in the United States of America

First Edition: February 2008

10 9 8 7 6 5 4 3 2 1

FaithWords is a division of Hachette Book Group USA, Inc. The FaithWords name and logo is a trademark of Hachette Book Group USA, Inc.

Library of Congress Cataloging-in-Publication Data

Blackston, Ray.
Par for the course / Ray Blackston. — 1st ed.
p. cm.
Summary: "Sparks fly when Ray Blackston returns with his trademark quirky sense of humor. Golf, politics, and romance collide in Par for the course; golf range owner Chris Hackett meets an attractive political correspondent who turns his world upside down"—Provided by the publisher
ISBN-13: 978-0-446-17815-0
ISBN-10: 0-446-17815-2
1. Golf stories. gsafd I. Title.
PS3602.L3255P37 2007
813'.6—dc22

2007009633

If a man digs a pit, he will fall into it.

—Proverbs 26:27 (NIV)

ACKNOWLEDGMENTS

Special thanks to my excellent editor, Anne Goldsmith, for her insight, advice, and encouragement. And a very appreciative hug to my agent, Beth Jusino, for finding a home for this project.

Par for the Course

1

LESSON FOR TODAY

Par has many meanings, and the
courses are often inside our heads.

I stood behind her in raw sunlight, my hands at her waist, urging her to turn slightly to the right. Without protest she did so. Mrs. Dupree lacked flexibility, though that is not what I would remember. Nor was it the private acre of grass on which we met each Tuesday afternoon. Nor was it the warm smell of salt marsh blowing in from across the bay. It was the way she accepted instruction.

"Like this?" she asked, and adjusted her stance.

"Yes," I replied. "For a beginner, you have an excellent golf swing. Just remember to turn fully and maintain a firm grip on the club."

Hack's Golf Learning Center was where Charleston's after-work crowd came to practice their technique. My sign hung above the entrance, and its wording was a natural offshoot of my last name: Hackett. Chris Hackett.

Mrs. Dupree fingered her 5-wood and looked past me at the driving range, where some twenty other adults were swatting away on fake grass mats, the "hitting mats," as customers referred to them. Striped range balls flew this way and that.

Mrs. Dupree turned to face me. "I've been wondering something, Chris."

"About your grip?"

"No, about you personally. You're so patient and understanding with your students, especially us women. There's no Mrs. Golfer on the horizon?"

This question popped up at least twice a week, and always from a female client. My answer never varied. "Thanks for the concern, Mrs. Dupree. But my teaching schedule and running this business consume my time, while my social life has been a series of relational double bogeys."

I said it in my best low country monotone, as if reciting the pledge of allegiance.

Fully half of my clientele were women, most of them beginners like Mrs. Dupree, who pounded three more balls at the 100-yard marker. Her stated goal was the same one pressing itself upon all my students—proficiency. She whacked her last ball, a slice that never rose more than three feet off the ground, and plunged her club back into her yellow golf bag. "Well, I just thought you might . . ." She hoisted her bag over her shoulder and turned to leave. "Oh, forget it. I'm intruding in your life."

I picked up the plastic range bucket and followed her along a sidewalk that curved behind the hitting mats. Several range hounds—my nickname for folks who showed up three or more times per week—paused from their practice and nodded their greetings as we passed. "You weren't intruding, Mrs. Dupree," I said in midstride. "It's just that I have so little time."

All who entered or exited Hack's had to walk across ten feet of green and white pea gravel. Maybe the fact that I followed Mrs. Dupree all the way through my golf shop and out across the gravel—*crunch, crunch*—to her Mercedes and loaded her golf bag into her trunk was a clue that I was interested in what she had to say.

She pressed a remote lock and her car doors snapped to attention. She spoke over the roof. "What I was going to say, Chris, was that someone I know is teaching a class on understanding the opposite sex. I thought it might be of interest to you."

My instinct was to grasp for an excuse, and I grasped hard. "But I have to be here at the Learning Center all day. No time for any classes."

She got in the car and lowered the passenger window. "It's a night class. The ad is in today's paper. Bottom of page B3."

Then she winked at me. But it wasn't a flirty wink, no, not at all; Mrs. Dupree was happily married. Her wink was the kind that says, "Listen to what I just told you. It might help."

Perhaps I needed help. In my experience there was something in the word "golf" or "golfer," or in the phrase "I teach golf" that repelled Southern women. (I had yet to date a Northerner.) For women here in Charleston, South Carolina, it was as if the word "golf" triggered preprogrammed objections to me as a potential mate. *He'll always be away on Saturday, whacking that little white ball with his buddies or teaching others to whack the little white ball, all the while ignoring me and the children.*

After Mrs. Dupree drove away, I forgot about her invitation and hurried back through my pro shop and out to the range. The middle section was elevated some ten feet, which gave beginners the illusion they could get a ball airborne. There I gave fifteen-minute lessons to two kids, an eight-year-old girl and her ten-year-old brother. Their father had signed them up and, surprisingly, urged me to be honest with them about their abilities. So I was. At the end of the lessons, I told the ten-year-old that his little sister could outdrive him with one hand tied behind her back.

The girl snickered. Their father told the boy to start pumping weights. The boy told his dad he preferred soccer. The kid even kicked a golf ball soccer-style and mumbled, "It ain't a sport unless you have to run after the ball."

At 7:30 p.m. the last hacker left Hack's. As was my habit at the end of a day, I stood behind the hitting mats and surveyed the acreage, looking for evidence of proficiency from my students. Then I noted the shot dispersion well right of the 100-yard and 150-yard markers. *Slicers, so many slicers.* Across the grass, thousands of golf balls lay scattered like summer hail refusing to melt.

I left the balls out there; they could be gathered the next morning. Inside my modest pro shop I counted the cash in the register and wrote out the next day's instructions for my groundskeeper. Next to the register sat today's paper, still rolled up and held with a rubber band. Curious, I pulled off the band and discarded all but section B. The ad centered on the bottom of page 3 read thusly:

Would you like to understand the opposite sex and learn why men often fail at communicating? Join my eight-week course! First session free; course cost $100. Meet in Conference Room #4 at the Hyatt, on Rivers Avenue. Tuesdays, 8:00 p.m. First meeting 9/06, hosted by Lin Givens. Hope to see you there!

I tore the ad from the page and tucked it into my shirt pocket, wondering if this Mr. Givens might be of help. I certainly had questions to bring; I wasn't shy. Understanding the intricacies of women's golf swings was one thing, but understanding women themselves…now this made my head hurt, a 5-iron to the skull.

Then I looked again at the ad. *September 6?*

Today was September 6.

Another glance at the clock. 7:53 p.m.

I locked the door to the pro shop, hurried to my truck, and sped for the Hyatt, pausing at stoplights to dab deodorant under each arm. My job entailed lots of sweating, and my spare container of Right Guard saved me on many occasions. My wardrobe check was even quicker. *Soiled khakis will have to do, as will the purple golf shirt.* Surely this meeting was informal. My effort at parking certainly was.

Pen in hand—taking notes was a priority—I strode across the Hyatt's lobby, thankful for good air-conditioning. A sign on the far wall shone in brass lettering:

CONFERENCE ROOM #4

I approached the door and noted an unusually sweet smell in the air. Even before I opened door number four and entered the room, I knew. My nostrils—soothed daily by the natural scent of Bermuda grass—told me that this evening I would be, no doubt, in the minority.

This is okay, I assured myself and reached for the door handle. *I'm thirty-one and single, a fairly confident guy. A room with a majority of nice-smelling women is fine, just fine.*

A woman's amplified voice boomed from inside. I turned the handle and pushed open the door.

Some sixty people, seated in eight rows of padded navy chairs, turned and stared.

Face flushing, I hurried through awkward silence to the empty back row and took a seat in the middle. From what I could tell, the attendees were taking turns introducing themselves.

I mouthed "sorry" to the two women who turned from row seven to eye me a second time. Then I checked my watch—8:19—and looked around for my fellow man.

No other males in sight. *I'm the only guy?*

At the front of the room sat a shallow stage carpeted in dark maroon. It supported a microphone stand, which supported a chrome mic, which the woman behind it gripped with great determination. She sported close-cropped hair and a gray pantsuit, and she looked positively peeved that someone had come late to her meeting.

She pointed at someone in row one. A woman stood and said, "Carly Thompson, media rep, Charleston," and sat down.

The next woman in the row stood and said, "Fran Tatum, owner of the Tatum Gallery, Hilton Head," and she too sat.

On the stage, the short-haired woman in the pantsuit nodded and pulled the mic to her lips. I noted her nametag, which read simply *LIN*.

"That should do it for our introductions," she said, "I believe we've covered everyone."

From the back row I waved my right arm, but she didn't see me. So I waved again. Her quick glance definitely was aimed my way, though it was only a glance. No nod. No "yes?" No "Your name, sir?" This woman downright ignored me.

I waved my arm a third time. No response.

If I had been a dog—spaniel or shepherd or poodle or labradoodle, it wouldn't have mattered—I'm certain the hair on my back would have stood up. In fact, I should have yelped, turned tail, and bolted. But I did not.

Sometimes it's the things you *don't do* that end up broadening your knowledge of the world, and what I didn't do was leave the room. No, at this point I was just a bit ticked that Ms. Speakerwoman had intentionally disregarded my tan, waving right arm. My competitive nature alone convinced me to remain planted.

"Okay, let's get to the subject of our talk today," Lin said next. "I assume you are all familiar with Eve and the fruit, are you not?" She peered back and forth at the first seven rows but never lifted her eyes to me.

A thin woman in the second row raised her hand. "You mean Eve and Adam and that apple thing?"

"Yes, Susan. That's correct."

Briefly I wondered why they were putting Eve before Adam. But then I forgot about the order of things, waved my arm a fourth time, and spoke from behind it. "I know the basics of that story too."

A few giggles from row five, but nothing from Lin. Perhaps a reddening of the complexion, as if further peeved at my presence. But no way was I leaving now. The newspaper ad had not specified *women only,* and besides, maybe I could learn something.

She gripped her mic again and gave it a slight twisting motion, as if to wrest it from its base. "Very well. Seems we are all versed in the storyline. You see, ladies, when Eve met the serpent—let's call him a snake, since that's what he was—she was already asserting her great power and independence."

"Tell it, sister," sounded a voice of affirmation in the first row.

Lin smiled around the side of her mic. "And the man, Adam—what was *he* doing? Genesis says the man was *with* her. Imagine that! Here is a man whose wife has been approached by a snake. And not just any snake, mind you, but a talking, manipulating snake! The man surely knows something is wrong, for he has never before encountered a verbose reptile."

"Neither have I," said the voice in the first row.

More giggles from row five.

"Same here," Lin said. "But back to our main issue. The man knows something is wrong, though he is apparently frozen with passivity. He simply leaves Eve to fend for herself. Can any of you relate?"

Heads nodded.

One whispered "amen."

Lin worked her audience, taking the time to make eye contact with many of the attendees. "I can certainly relate," she said. "Adam ignores her! He's a bystander, a mere spectator while this talking snake tries to con his wife. What *should* the man have done?"

Offended but amused, I leaned back in my chair until my head rested against the wall. *A man-hater quoting from the Bible? How weird is this?*

"Anyone?" Lin asked the room. "What should the man have done?"

A woman stood in the fourth row. She turned, and I read her nametag: *CECELIA*.

Obviously enthused about the subject matter, Cecelia put her hands on her ample hips and said, "What that man shoulda done, at a bare minimum, is hold up his hands to the snake and say, 'Mister Snake, now you just hold on a second. Just zip your serpent lip, 'cause I need to talk to my wife.'"

"That's mostly correct, Cecelia," Lin said from the stage. "If Adam had information that would have helped Eve, he should have told her beforehand, stepped away, and then allowed Eve to independently make the decision. She was fully capable of doing the right thing; she just needed a tad more info."

Cecelia waved her arm, which was immediately acknowledged. "But that man, Adam, he didn't do nothin'! He just stood there and watched. Uh-huh, just stood there and watched it all fall apart."

Lin was by now grinning over the mic. "And then...THEN the man points the finger at the woman and tells God, 'She did it!'"

"Yep, just like a man."

"Bingo" and "Preach it, sister" emanated from the room.

"Wait a second!" I interrupted. Heads turned, none smiling. "Are you saying the man, Adam, was merely a supplier of information to Eve, who would have not eaten the fruit if she'd had 'just a tad more info'? That's ridiculous."

"Ridiculous to you, perhaps." And again Lin refused to look at me.

Her ongoing effort to overlook me produced a certain boldness in me. Without so much as a raise of my hand I blurted, "Hey, Miss Lin Givens, you haven't even let me introduce myself yet. Why the cold shoulder?"

She shrugged with a kind of mock sympathy before sharing an embarrassed smile with women in the first two rows. "Okay then, sir, tell us. Tell us who you are."

"You mean you're letting me introduce myself?"

"Please."

I leaned forward and gripped the chair in front of me, unsure if I should stand. "I'm Chris Hackett, and I own and operate Hack's Golf Learning Center, west of the Ashley River, here in Charleston." Then I sensed the need to say more, to make them comfortable with my presence. "I appreciate y'all allowing a man in the class. I figure this male-female stuff is kinda like learning the golf swing. You have to grasp the fundamentals before you make meaningful progress."

Lin cocked her head to the side. Then her expression changed slowly from amusement to confusion to sarcastic nod.

"Ah, yes... *golf*," she said to her cohorts in the first row, "yet another example of male dominance. And what do we think our dear Eve would have done with the sport?"

Women in seven rows looked at each other as if pondering the correct answer. I knew the correct answer, though I wanted to hear what the females might say. Lin scanned her congregation and repeated loudly, "Ladies, what do we think our dear Eve would have done with the sport?"

"Bit the forbidden golf ball?" I asked. "Cracked a tooth?"

Oh, the tension in that room. Oh, the turned heads and raised eyebrows. Oh, how Lin's personality grated against mine. And oh, how I hoped she didn't carry a concealed weapon.

What she carried was a degree of arrogance that was rare for the genteel city of Charleston. "Are you a member of a country club, Mr. Hackett?" she inquired.

"Yes, I am. Yeamans Hall Club."

Lin looked again to the first row, which I figured was filled with her yes-women. "You'll notice, ladies, the root words of the country club to which Chris belongs—'yeah' and 'man,' as if that very name was invented to secretly cheer themselves on."

Steam filled my shirt. I couldn't take any more. "But you just don't know—"

Lin raised both hands to halt me in midsentence. "Are there any women members at the Yeah-man's Hall Golf Club, Mr. Hackett?"

I squirmed in my seat. "Um, I'm not... Yeah, I think so."

"You're not sure?"

"Okay, yes, I've definitely seen some women playing at the club."

Tenacity was not just her middle name; it must have been emblazoned on her family coat of arms. "And how many of those women have you played golf with in the past year?"

I shook my head in disbelief. "I don't think I've actually *played* with any. But I did give free lessons to a woman at my practice range last month. She was poor. A single mom."

Sarcasm must have been emblazoned just below tenacity. "You don't say . . ."

I noted her pale left hand and compared it to her tan right one. This woman was a golfer, and she wore a glove when she played. My competitive instinct kicked in again and together with the emotion of the moment caused me to blurt, "Yeah, and one more thing: If you'd care to meet me at a course and play an 18-hole round, I'll make you a bet."

"A bet? At *golf*?" Amusement had returned, at least in her tone of voice.

I felt the burden of defending all males on planet Earth. "Yep, at golf. You can play from the red tees, and I'll spot you ten strokes for the eighteen holes. If I win, I get half of the teaching time for this class of yours, meaning that I share the stage with you and get to promote the male perspective on all this relational stuff."

A buzz filled the room—a decidedly feminine buzz.

"And if I win," Lin said with confidence, "you complete the eight-week course as the sole male in the room, and you get no stage time at all, and you have to sit right here in the front row." She pointed to her first-row friends.

Again sixty heads turned toward me, few of them smiling. One older lady seated in front of me whispered, "Do it, sonny. Take the bet!"

Somewhere above row four, my gaze and Lin's met in fiery battle.

"Deal," I said.

"Deal," she replied. "Thursday at two?"

"At Yeamans Hall Club?"

She nodded. "I'll bring my own caddy."

For the last fifteen minutes of class Lin continued to extol the virtues of Eve and mock the actions of Adam. When finally she dismissed us, none of the others made an attempt to speak to me. To be fair, I didn't seek them out either. I wasn't scared of being offended again, or ignored, or even disrespected. No, what consumed me as I walked out of the Hyatt that night was why Lin Givens sounded so confident in making a golf bet with a professional instructor.

2

LESSON FOR TODAY

The grip is all that attaches you to the golf club.
The proper grip utilizes the fingers of the hands
more than the palms. With a proper grip of the
club (or proper grip of any subject matter), one
can spare oneself much embarrassment, such as
outright whiffs and ill-timed wagers.

At seven in the morning—my usual start time—I arrived at
Hack's and saw my golf range absent of a single ball. In the dew
covering all that Bermuda, tire tracks curved, crisscrossed, and
backtracked. No worries, however. These tracks were not from
a thief's car but from my own golf cart.

Cack Pruitt, my sixty-year-old greenkeeper, had arrived early
and gathered the balls with what he called his range-picker.
The range-picker was a kind of rolling retrieval system hitched
to the back of a golf cart. I owned two carts—this plain one and
one Cack had customized.

This morning Cack toiled on his knees, applying grease to
an axle. An oily red rag protruded from the back pocket of his
jeans and a dirty ball cap had collapsed on his head.

"Mornin', Cack," I shouted from the back door of the pro
shop.

"Just greasin' your range cart, Mister Pro," he said without looking up. "If I don't do it, it'll never get done."

Cack routinely solved the world's problems, usually while sipping a Mountain Dew in the shade of his dilapidated umbrella table. He'd brought the umbrella table down from Myrtle Beach after I hired him, telling me his wife had given him the thing for an anniversary present some twenty years earlier. The umbrella table was faded blue on one side and dirty white on the other. It sat teetering on the far right side of the range, surrounded by three plastic chairs. He called this area the Groundskeeper's Café. Though Cack would let anyone sit and listen, he took no reservations. Whoever sat there got to listen to Cack's version of what was wrong with planet Earth and its billions of inhabitants.

The previous week he'd waxed on about the Middle East to my customers—if we don't protect the oil, somebody else will steal it; we should give polygraph tests twice a day to each member of Congress; TV networks hire too many good-looking anchorwomen, which distracts him from the actual news. Followed by the state of golf in general—too many scientists and metallurgists involved, inventing clubs that knock the ball ten miles, and this has made the game too easy.

Cack didn't play golf himself, but he'd get almost teary-eyed telling you how he missed the days of persimmon club heads, custom sanded and polished by expert craftsmen.

Weekday mornings were slow at Hack's—we were hoping to get some elementary school field trips booked in the near future—and this allowed ample time for small talk with my coworker. After opening the pro shop and checking my lesson schedule, I wandered out behind the hitting mats and down to where Cack had taken up residence in his three-seat café. I carried a cold Mountain Dew, which I handed him without greeting.

"Tuesdays are your night for runnin' the picker-upper," he said in an accusative tone. Seated in his plastic chair, he opened the canned drink and faced the rising sun, which reflected white and bronze in his chin stubble.

I sat across the rickety table from him and stretched my legs. "I know. I'll run the picker tonight. Last night I had, um, a class."

Cack sipped his Dew, wiped his mouth with his forearm. "You taking another business class? I thought you were done with that."

"I am. This was…a different kind of class."

I hoped he'd let the subject pass, but Cack was about as likely to let a subject pass as he was to turn down a free Mountain Dew.

"Then what, boss man, are you doing in a class if you've already finished your business degree?"

I plucked a broken tee from the ground and used its tip to clean my thumbnail. "Nothin' much. Just a little course on relationships."

"Aw, don't go telling me you went to that thing at the Hyatt, what Mrs. Glen told me about. Something about understanding why men and women can't communicate. That's the one, ain't it?"

I nodded. "That's the one, Caskster. Only it's a slam against men, taught by a man-hater. I was the only male in the room."

My guess was next Cack would ask me how many females were in the room.

He thumped a fingernail against the can once, then again. "How many women?"

"About sixty."

"So you left, right? Couldn't stand up to the man-hater?"

"Um, no. Actually I made an attempt to defend the entire male gender."

He was grinning now, and the gold in his left molar shown brightly in the sunlight. "And she put you in your place?"

"She tried. Actually she blames Adam for all the problems women have in the world."

Cack took another swig of Dew. He looked confused. "Adam? He that guy running for state senator? Lives in Beaufort?"

"No, Cack. I meant the original Adam...the fruit thing, with Eve."

He tilted his drink can high and gulped the balance. Then he dropped the can on the ground and stomped it flat with his work shoe. "Let me get this straight. You stayed for a class that was all women, which is taught by a man-hater, and she blames Adam for thousands of years of women's problems?"

"I did, it is, and she does."

He winced and tugged his cap low on his head. "You're gonna make me ask why you stayed, aren't ya?"

"Actually I was hoping we could change the subject to why the crabgrass is creeping into the Bermuda on our range."

Cack slowly shook his head. "I'll take care of the grass. You just tell me why you stayed for that class if it was taught by a man-hater."

I rocked back on the legs of my chair, debating between a lie and some altered version of the truth. "I might not have a choice. You see, Cack, I sorta got mad, and when I get mad I tend to get—"

"Very competitive. I know 'bout that."

"Yeah, so I sorta made a bet with the lady."

He shook his head in disbelief. "What kind of bet?"

"A golf bet, of course."

"You WHAT?!" He nearly jumped out of his chair. Instead he leaned across the table and tried scolding me with just his stare. When that didn't work well enough, he resorted to verbiage. "You made a golf bet with a *feminist*? Son, she's gonna have all her buddies out there lining the fairways! They'll taunt you while you try to putt. They'll call you a male bigot in the middle of your backswing. You're gonna shoot a one hundred, Chris. You'll be *lucky* to break one hundred. Heck, you might shoot a two hundred."

I took the double scolding about as well as I could, given the circumstances. He was right—I should've kept my mouth shut.

After he'd berated me a third time, I rose from my chair and looked down at him. "I only have one question for you, Cackster."

"Name it."

"Will you be my caddy?"

The sound of pea gravel crunching under customers' golf shoes meant business was good. And now, after six years of ownership, I could sometimes even tell by the sound whether the cruncher was male or female.

The males showed up first. That afternoon I gave lessons to four guys from the Charleston shipyards. Big, burly guys in jeans and T-shirts, arms the size of cypress trunks. They were raw beginners. Enthusiastic, raw beginners. All they wanted to do was hit balls with a driver and hit them as far as possible. They'd whiff one, shank one, top one, then hit one clear over the fence at the end of my driving range. The sign at the base read 315 yards, a colossal poke by any standards.

When they were done—"I should enter long-drive contests!" was the biggest guy's boast—they each gave me forty bucks in cash and left laughing, bragging to one another about the length of their shots but agreeing that the sport of golf was way too expensive.

At five-thirty a very different kind of new student showed up: Female. Thirtyish. Slender. Auburn streaks in shoulder-length brown hair. No ring. Big smile.

"You're Chris?" she asked, striding past hitting mats four and five, a teal-colored golf bag slung over her shoulder.

I was setting out buckets of balls for Happy Hour and thinking about tomorrow's bet with Lin Givens. To receive a warm greeting was both welcome and stunning. Kneeling on the mat with a hundred golf balls, I fumbled for words.

"I'm, um, yes, I'm Chris. And you must be Molly, my five-thirty lesson?"

She set her golf bag down a few feet behind the hitting mat.

"I am." And before I could say anything else, she pulled a club from her bag, slipped a golf glove on to her left hand, and stepped up on the hitting mat. "Okay, Mister Chris, where do we start?"

Just what I craved from students. Enthusiasm.

The lesson went fine—she quickly grasped the concept of the correct grip and was learning the swing plane—until she requested something that few students ever request. She asked to see me hit a few.

"I'm very visual," Molly said between practice swings. "If I see the swing of someone who's good, I'll learn faster."

I borrowed her 7-iron, stepped on to the hitting mat, and took two practice swings. Then I aimed at the 150-yard marker and hit a ball that landed just feet from the marker's base.

A simple "nice shot" was the response one might expect. What I got was silence.

Molly sat on the grass directly behind me, looking down the line of my aim, her eyes scrunched as if not quite understanding what she'd just witnessed.

"One more," she said. "Swing just like that one more time."

I rolled another ball onto the mat with the club head. I hit this one much like the first and watched it land some five yards right of the marker.

"Just one more," Molly said. "I almost have it."

I tried not to laugh when I said, "A beginner who can grasp all the nuances of the swing from watching three shots from her instructor is a rare bird indeed."

"Tweet tweet," she said, focusing in as I prepared to hit another ball.

Her manner impressed me as a combination of comic banter and girlish curiosity. Just as attractive was how studious she became while watching me swing. She remained directly behind me, some five feet away, staring intently down the line to the target.

I hit the third ball, watched it land just left of the marker, and turned to gauge her reaction.

Big smile. "I got it now. Can I try?"

In hindsight, what I should have done was simply hand her the 7-iron, trade places with her, and encourage her as I did all my new students. But I was thinking about the bet tomorrow with Lin Givens, who seemed to be everything that this Molly was not.

She was harsh; Molly was curious.

She ignored me; Molly grinned often.

She despised men; Molly, from what I could tell, knew the art of subtle flirting.

"Do ya mind," I asked, still on the mat, "if I hit a couple more? I have a match tomorrow and could use the practice. I won't charge these minutes to your lesson."

Her eyes grew wide. "A match?! Really? You compete against other men pros for trophies and things?"

Her interest and enthusiasm flattered me to the eighteenth degree.

"Well, sometimes," I blushed. Somewhere between those two words humility strained to break forth. "But tomorrow's bet is with a woman. We met yesterday and had a discussion that culminated in a wager."

Her smile and curiosity wilted like unwatered zoysia.

"You gamble against *women students*? For money?" She reached out and took her 7-iron from my hands, as if reconsidering her lesson. "What kind of a teacher are you?"

I shouldn't have snickered, but the sound from my mouth as I looked over her shoulder and noted the dozens of people arriving for Happy Hour was close to a snicker. "I don't think you understand. The woman I have a bet with is a radical, a true man-hater."

Molly shook her head and set her 7-iron back into her golf bag. "You just met the woman yesterday, and you've already branded her sexist *and* you're betting money with her? How can you bet money with beginning students or label people that fast?"

I saw the confusion and did my best to explain. "Well…it's not really like that. There was this class, and she offended me, offended me greatly, and . . ."

Her three steps away told me she was not buying this. I was so bad at this kind of thing.

She backed farther away, hoisting her bag over her shoulder. "I'm sorry, Chris, but gambling just repels me. I watched it ruin the life of someone close to me. And anyway, I think I've learned enough swing tips for today. I'll leave my check on your counter." Then she turned and strode toward my pro shop.

For a moment I chastised myself for even bringing up the subject. "Wait, Molly, you don't understand. I never gamble with . . ." But she was already through the exit.

"Students," I said to nothing but air.

Before I could even process disappointment, Cack rang the Happy Hour bell, and I hurried to the pro shop to greet golf-happy Charlestonians.

By 6:15, thirty of the thirty-six range mats were occupied, as well as the majority of the Bermuda grass hitting area to the right side. I made my way slowly down the range, offering free swing tips, saying hello to longtime customers. Happy Hour lured all kinds—men and women in corporate casual, kids in shorts, teenagers in who knows what fashion, all swatting ball after ball and counting down the minutes to 6:44 p.m.

At 6:44 each Wednesday, a heightened sense of excitement came over my Learning Center. At 6:44 I ducked inside my pro shop, grabbed a bullhorn from behind the counter, and came back out with the thing pressed firmly to my lips.

"Ladies and gentlemen, kids and hackers," I announced, "please stop hitting for a moment and turn your attention to the maintenance shed. It's time to play Whack the Cack!"

Claps and whistles filled the range. Heads turned to face the maintenance shed. And out from the shed came Cack, driving his custom, metal-caged golf cart and waving from behind half-inch wire mesh. The cage was shaped like a top hat, which gave the cart a kind of Mad Hatter appearance. A clown face painted on the front of the cart, a red bull's eye on each side and a third one on the back, added to the unconventional look.

Cack drove up to the mats, greeted a group of teenagers, and waved me over. Through the metal door of his cart I handed him the bullhorn. Without a word he took off for the 100-yard marker. Customers cheered and pulled from their bags 5-irons, drivers, 3-woods, whatever club that gave the most confidence.

Cack drove out to the middle of the range and wheeled the cart around to face the hitting mats. From inside his caged cart he raised the bullhorn and shouted in his best low country drawl, "All right, you bunch of hackers, hit me and you win a free bucket of balls."

He took off on the cart, doing long figure eights across the Bermuda. Though he'd never admitted it to me, he'd tweaked the engine as well; his cart was extraordinarily fast.

White pellets flew through the air, most very wide of the moving target. Balls rolled on the ground. Balls skidded at odd angles. Others launched straight up, like a pop fly.

Cack zigged and zagged across the range, weaving the cart and shouting, "You folks shoot like Union soldiers drunk on moonshine!"

This was the South, and that sort of comment riled Southerners. In fact, some got in such a hurry to swing that they missed the ball completely, or hit the mat first and sent the ball dribbling only a few feet.

Cack laughed at them through his bullhorn and shouted, "I've seen one-armed baboons swing a golf club better than you people!"

This was Cack's favorite line, and for some reason it infuriated male golfers. One guy out on mat number thirty got so ticked that he tossed a club, helicopter-style, out onto the range. It landed far behind the moving cart while the people around him roared at his frustration. Women, for the most part, laughed off Cack's frequent insults, but men and boys just kept firing away, determined to wallop their antagonist.

For males, I believe this was a kind of "play army" event, whereby instead of paintball guns their weaponry consisted of clubs and golf balls. Something primal triggers when Southern males encounter a moving target.

Cack would not let up. "The guy on hitting mat number five swings like a little girl!"

The guy turned three shades of red and began firing away as fast as he could hit the balls, most of them shanks and dribbles.

All this, of course, was great for business; I wish I could claim the idea as my own. But the idea had arrived years earlier with Cack and his dilapidated umbrella table. He'd spent his second day on the job with a welding mask on his head and a welding torch in his hands, forming the top hat and mounting the curved, cylindrical pieces to the sides of the cart. He explained to me that, for most people, a driving range was a place to vent, to let go of frustrations formed from the difficulties of life. His bullhorn antics served to play off that frustration while adding humor as a balm, not to mention adding lots of revenue for the business. If only finding Mrs. Golfer were so easy.

"Look at that teenage girl on mat number twelve!" shouted Cack as he looped around the 100-yard marker. "She ought to stay home and knit sweaters like her great grandmaw!"

In mock anger, the teenager and her three friends picked up handfuls of balls and threw them at the cart.

Some guy near the end of the range finally hit a low shot that bounced into Cack's cage. *Thwop.*

Cack was quick with the bullhorn. "Give that man a free bucket of balls, Chris!" he shouted. "Then tell 'im he got lucky. Tell 'im he couldn't hit the ocean from the deck of the Queen Mary."

The insanity continued, and people ran from the mats to my pro shop window to buy extra buckets of balls. No employee worked the window, mind you; for Happy Hour we employed the honor system—a bright yellow bucket on which I'd written the rules with a Sharpie pen. HONOR SYSTEM: 2 BUCKETS FOR $7

Next thing I knew, Cack called a twenty-second time out. Two kids ran out onto the range, climbed into the passenger side of the cart, and shut the metal door. Off went the threesome in the rolling top hat, the kids squealing, Cack turning in wild circles. "INCOMING!" he shouted from the bullhorn, and *bang,* another ball careened off the metal cage.

By 8:00 p.m. darkness had descended, and my once boisterous grounds sat quiet and scarred, the grass wounded from the frantic swings of happy customers. This contrast, the sheer silence when the grounds were empty, always amazed me.

Cack and I closed the range, and in a solemn half hour we picked up the balls and dumped them into plastic drums to be used again the next day. That's what I loved about the business of golf balls—they're reusable, low maintenance, and never file claims of unfair labor practices.

At the pro shop counter I gathered with my groundskeeper to count the night's haul. From the cash in the yellow bucket we determined we'd sold one hundred and forty-two buckets of practice balls in an hour and a half. In this business, five hundred bucks was a good day, a very good day. I tipped the Cackster sixty bucks and bid him good night.

"Next Wednesday evening, I wanna drive the cart," I said as he made his way to the exit.

He pushed the glass door open and spoke over his shoulder. "You're not funny enough."

Alone in my shop now, I locked the register and pulled two notes from under a paperweight. People were always leaving me notes, asking me to call them to arrange lessons for junior, wanting me to repair a club. I pulled out the first note and held it under the overhead light.

Chris,

Tonight during Wack da Kack I ran out of golf balls and money. So I'm leaving this IOU for a bucket of balls. You know I'm good for it!

    Mark McMellon (poor freshman at Wando High School)

The other note was written in loopy, female handwriting.

Chris,

I may have overreacted today during my lesson. I recently broke up with a guy who was heavily involved with gambling, so I guess I freaked out a bit. Anyway, I hope you win your bet with your man-hating golf student. And since I'm paying for a 3-lesson package, I'll contact you in the next day or so.
   Happy golfing,
   Molly

Her check for $110 lay under her note. I stuffed the check and both notes into my pocket, but reconsidered and drew out the note from the high school kid. After reading it a second time, I tossed it into the trash. I was once a poor teenager.

The last thing I did every night before locking the shop was to shut down my work computer. Hand on mouse, I let curiosity about tomorrow's opponent get the best of me, so into the Yahoo! search engine I typed, "Lin Givens, women's rights."

The second match startled me.

Lin Givens…women's rights activist…lecturer…MBA from Brown, 1988…three-year letterwoman, women's golf…political campaign volunteer…political aspirations…

Though the lights over my range had long been turned off—all six banks of them—this new data forced me to relight the Bermuda.

Minutes later under the bright rays of the light poles, I emptied five buckets of range balls into a sort of sloppy pyramid. Focused and resolute, I determined to stay out here till midnight if that's what it took to hone my game. I would aim and strike every one of the practice balls until Ms. Lin Givens had no chance.

I set my golf bag next to the pyramid and began practice with an 8-iron.

One after another I raked the balls onto a level patch of grass, aimed, and fired. White pellets launched high into night air, bright and rising, then faded in the darkness and descended to earth.

Thwack. *I don't care if Lin played collegiate golf.*

Thwack. *I'll embarrass her just like she embarrassed me.*

Thwack. *But what if she really is good?*

Thwack. *Why'd I open my big mouth and spot her ten strokes for an eighteen-hole match?*

Sweat poured from me on this hot September night.

Thwack. *I'm glad Molly is coming back for more lessons.*

Thwack. *Don't get distracted by thoughts of Molly.*

Thwack. *Molly is really cute. And personable.*

Thwack.

Thwack.

Thwack.

3

LESSON FOR TODAY

A proper stance will help one swing the club in balance. And balance, of course, is the key to rhythm. So never seek to copy an opponent's poor stance (or obnoxious behavior), as this will surely ruin one's rhythm.

The entrance to Yeamans Hall Country Club always reminded me of a dirt road into a nineteenth century plantation. Along each side of the entrance, Spanish moss hung from monstrous oak limbs, its shade random and intimidating. These trees and the dappled light that pierced them were all that greeted us as I mentally prepared for my opponent—an opponent whose skill level I had neither seen nor estimated.

"Nervous?" Cack asked from the passenger seat of my truck.

I shook my head no, turned behind the whitewashed clubhouse, and parked beneath yet another overgrown oak. Dozens of vehicles lined the lot, unusual for a Thursday afternoon.

I checked in at the golf shop and greeted the assistant pro, Joey, who was sorting merchandise behind the counter. He looked up and said, "Howdy, Chris. I hear you made a bet."

"Just a small one, Joey. Just a small one." I signed my name on the members pad and grabbed a handful of tees from the freebie box.

Joey leaned across the counter and looked down at what I'd written on the pad. "Um, Chris, you'll have to pay for your guest."

"Cack?" I answered, surprised at the request. "He's only cad-dying for me. He doesn't even play golf."

"I meant the woman you're playing against. She checked in twenty minutes ago and said you'd take care of the greens fees. She's out on the practice range, warming up."

Paying her way was the first of several indignities. "Just put her fee on my tab," I said and turned for the door.

He did, but not without further comment. "Oh, and you should know something else."

"Yeah?"

"She brought friends."

I left the shop and muttered "great" as I caught up to Cack, who slung my golf bag over his shoulder and strode toward the practice range. White sneakers adorned his feet, and a Yea-mans cap sat low on his head. He seemed content in his role as caddie.

I opted for the same khaki pants and golf shirt—purple—that I'd worn to Lin's class. Fresh-washed and matched to my cap, the shirt broadcast a subtle message: Purple was the color of royalty, and I fully intended to show Lin who was king.

In my eagerness to get to the range and warm up, however, I had failed to notice how sore I was from hitting five buckets of balls the previous night. I made slow swinging motions to stretch my back and arms. *Ouch.*

Cack and I eased between a pair of holly bushes and saw out on the range some thirty women gathered around a lone player—Lin, dressed in black, and hitting balls with a fairway wood. Her swing was impressive; her gallery, unexpected. She was only practicing, and still they clapped for her every shot.

"This should be an interesting day," Cack mumbled, setting my bag upright some twenty yards left of Lin and her groupies.

I hit only fifteen balls during my warm up. Five with a wedge, five with a 6-iron, and five with a driver. On the surface this may have looked like a routine; in reality it was my attempt to hide anxiety.

Cack and I spent twenty minutes on the putting green, gauging its speed, holing lots of six-footers. The course had just been watered, and from the moist turf steam rose in waves, the smell of fertilizer strong in its wake.

Confident and ready for battle, we strode to the first tee, where Lin and her minions stood waiting. They parted slightly to allow Cack and me into the tee box, then filled in around us. Lin stood ten feet away, rubbing a golf ball in her hands. Her body language—she was half-turned to the left, away from us—told me that an offer to shake hands would be futile. Still, I at least wanted to appear relaxed and conversational.

"You didn't tell me you played golf at Brown University," I said, reaching into the bottom pocket of my golf bag for a new ball.

"Well, Chris, you didn't ask."

I glanced at Cack. He shrugged and rolled his eyes.

Seconds later I caught Joey, the assistant pro, peering out of the golf shop window, his hands shielding the glare from his eyes. A man-versus-woman match at Yeamans Hall was a rarity. I imagined even the cooks and cart boys had been alerted to the game.

Then, right there on the first tee, in a setting that demands courtesy and respect toward one's opponent, the chants started: "Yeah woman! Yeah woman! Yeah woman!"

This continued for a loud two minutes. Ignored again, I moved between the tee markers—the blue markers—and prepared to hit my first shot. I would play first, as the blue tees sat fifty yards behind the red tees, from which Lin would start.

While I took practice swings, two of the chanters slapped high-fives with Lin, the chantee. Overconfidence abounded.

Cack pointed to his watch. 2:02 p.m. "Let's get started," he whispered into my ear. "Just stay calm, don't let the groupies bother you, and put a smooth swing on your golf ball."

While teeing my ball, I tried to remember all three of his pointers. I was so eager to get started, however, that the thought registered in my head as, *Don't let the calm groupie swing smoothly.*

Then, as if my equipment had sided with the opposition, my ball decided to fall off its wooden peg. I smiled with embarrassment and reteed the ball.

I took my stance and prepared to hit my first shot. As always, I inhaled and blew the air out through my nose. But just as I was about to swing, Lin cleared her throat and said, "Remember that I get ten strokes."

Without taking my eye off my golf ball I muttered, "I remember."

Then, "I haven't played golf in a month."

"That's because you've been too busy demonizing men," I said just a split second before I lashed the ball down the middle of the fairway.

No one applauded. Except Cack, of course. He clapped loudly, much too loudly. He even whistled before blurting, "That's the way to hit it like a *man*."

I handed him my club and whispered, "Try not to overdo it. We don't want them calling for reinforcements. Thirty raging feminists is plenty."

Lin's gallery—some of them carried poster-board signs, one of which was a homemade scoreboard—followed her ahead to the red tee markers. The scoreboard listed the first nine holes on one side, the second nine on the other. I shook my head at its lettering:

	#1	#2	#3	#4	#5	#6	#7	#8	#9
The Great Eve:									
Passive Adam:									

Lin played the game with quickness and efficiency—she teed her ball, aimed, and swung. Her swing was not powerful, but from this first shot she proved very accurate.

She and her gallery strode ahead on the fairway. Cack and I trailed behind, speculating on any hijinks to come.

"You worried?" he asked me.

I noted the squishy nature of the turf at Yeamans, a well-watered layout that sat next to the Goose Creek wetlands. The fairways here always seemed warm and hospitable, in contrast to our opponent, who was neither. "Of course I'm worried. Anytime no one in a gallery claps for a good shot, I get worried." I tried to picture Molly clapping for me, but the vision grew hazy.

The chanters started up again, this time for at least a full minute. Cack and I walked on for another fifteen paces, doing our best to concentrate on the task at hand. He stooped to pluck a few blades of grass, tossing them overhead to test the wind. We agreed that breezes were negligible, but then he turned his attention back to the all-female gallery. "Think any of 'em belong to a gang?" he asked.

For several paces I let the question linger, preferring instead to watch a stray cloud hide the sun. "Just because most of 'em are wearing black? Don't be silly. They've probably all been disappointed by the men in their lives, and so today, golf is their comeuppance."

"Never heard you use a word like 'comeuppance.'"

"Just carry the bag, Cack."

He tromped another twenty yards before whispering out the side of his mouth, "You always use big words like 'comeuppance' when you get nervous."

We avoided walking too close to Lin and her gallery, preferring to stay on the opposite side of the fairway. She hit her second shot much like her first—with little hesitation and a resolute demeanor. With her fairway wood she knocked the ball straight at the pin. The ball landed in the fringe of the green and bounded onto the surface, some thirty feet from the hole.

I said, "Good shot." But she just marched on toward the green, putter in hand.

Cack handed me my 6-iron and shook his head. "Pitiful," he muttered. "Can't even acknowledge 'good shot.'"

Pride was at stake on both sides, and somehow, even at this early stage of the match, I was certain that I could take losing better than Lin. Everything about her, from her walk to her cold no-handshake greeting on the first tee, broadcasted how seriously she viewed our bet.

Not that I expected to lose, just that the concept was not foreign to me. During the two years I played college golf at the University of Georgia, I had practiced often with members of both the men's and the women's team. One young woman from Texas, a soft-spoken girl named Sue, beat me as often as I beat her. Competition at that level far outweighed gender bias; if someone was good and wanted to play a match, you played. We played for pizzas, and we paid up with a smile.

The camaraderie still lingered. Years after I'd forgotten who won what tournament and who shot what score, it is the road trips with golf buddies, the surprisingly good meals at hole-in-the-wall restaurants, that glue themselves in memory.

This was what I was thinking about as I stood over my ball. Well, that and wondering if Molly liked pizza.

And this is probably why I pulled the shot into a sand bunker. White grains splashed at the ball's entry. I winced, knowing that if I was already spotting Lin ten strokes, I didn't need to make such dumb mistakes.

Cack took the club from me and wiped the grass off the clubface. "You seemed distracted over that shot," he said. "Like you were in another world."

"I was. I was back in college...ordering pizzas."

He sighed and slung the bag strap over his shoulder. "You best forget pizzas and remember where you are. You gotta defend the male gender, remember? Ain't that what you told me?"

I replaced my divot, stomped it with my foot, and agreed. "Sure...the entire male gender."

Minutes later I blasted my ball from the sand but took two putts to get the ball in the hole. A score of 5. A bogey. No sound from the gallery.

Lin putted her ball to three feet away. Then she tapped it into the hole. A score of 4. A par. Her gallery burst into wild applause. Not polite applause or cordial applause, but wild, biased cheering.

Cack set the flagstick back into the hole and followed me to my golf bag. "Pretty rude and inappropriate to cheer that loudly, eh?"

"By now, Cackster, nothing surprises me."

By losing the first hole by one shot, I had in effect now spotted Lin eleven strokes—and had only seventeen more holes in which to make up the deficit.

This fact was affirmed by a member of Lin's gallery, who held up the homemade scoreboard and waved it for all to see. She had just updated the scores in black Magic Marker.

On the way to the second tee, Lin strode ahead of me and spoke over her shoulder. "You're now eleven strokes behind."

"I know that."

During the next five holes, her effort at conversation remained nil. I gained back two strokes in this stretch, though I was still nine behind when we teed off on #7. Thus after six holes the mobile scoreboard looked like this:

	#1	#2	#3	#4	#5	#6	#7	#8	#9
The Great Eve:	4	4	5	6	3	4			
Passive Adam:	5	4	5	4	4	3			

With the chants growing louder in between shots—Lin's gallery seemed to sense a struggle—we matched scores on the next two holes.

"Wonder what they'd call me if *I* were competing?" Cack asked as he toted the golf bag to the ninth tee.

"Passive Adam's crazy sexist uncle?"

His reply was purely Cackish. "Just hit your little white ball, Adam."

By the time we reached the fairway on the ninth hole—a longish par five—I had labeled Lin's game decent in some aspects and good in others, such as putting and driving accuracy. But she had yet to hit a ball into a sand bunker, and when finally she did this on her third shot to the green—plunging her ball deep into a cavernous half acre of sand—her gallery gasped.

Inexplicably, Lin took six strokes to get her ball out of that bunker. Sand flew everywhere. She chopped at that ball as if it were the poisonous male cousin of the talking snake.

She'd taken three shots to get *into* the sand, six to get out, and then two putts on the green. I made a birdie. Thus as we completed the first nine holes, the scoreboard looked like this:

	#1	#2	#3	#4	#5	#6	#7	#8	#9	Total
The Great Eve:	4	4	5	6	3	4	5	4	11	46
Passive Adam:	5	4	5	4	4	3	5	4	4	38

Her blunder had allowed me to make up eight strokes of the ten-stroke deficit, which gave me at least some degree of confidence. Now, halfway into the match, Passive Adam felt he could show some initiative in this garden of Bermuda and salt marsh.

Or could he?

What happened next can only be blamed on the serpent's visit to the Carolina low country. Here the talking snake had reconnected with Eve and imputed into her his favorite agenda—personal gain and blatant manipulation.

The TV reporter stopped me beneath a mammoth oak, somewhere between the ninth green and the tenth tee. She was a blonde in an electric blue skirt, and I had not noticed her in the gallery. Her bright outfit and long blonde hair would surely have stood out among all that black. But there she came with microphone in hand, slithering tongue in mouth, saying she wanted to ask me a few questions. At first I figured the assistant pro, Joey, was just having some fun and had called a friend from the local news.

But the lady's first question told me I was wrong about her motivation. She pulled the microphone to her lips and made an "okay" signal with her left hand. That's when I noticed a camerawoman had crept up behind us.

I elbowed Cack, who was standing beside me with the golf bag still on his shoulder, trying to make sense of the media invasion. *Channel 8 News?* There was no Channel 8 News in Charleston.

The reporter smiled at the camera and said, "I have with me one Chris Hackett, owner of Hack's Golf Learning Center here in Charleston."

I nodded, appreciative of her identifying my name and business early in the interview. Great for advertising, I figured.

But then her tone changed.

"Is it not true, Mr. Hackett, that once a week you encourage your customers—including many teenagers—to strike golf balls with the intention of hitting someone in a moving golf cart?"

Beside me holding the golf bag upright, Cack cocked his head to the side, eyes wide with surprise. I looked at Cack and did likewise before turning my attention back to the reporter. "Well it's not quite like that, ma'am. You see—"

"The cart *is* moving, is it not, Mr. Hackett?" Her expression was stern. Her camerawoman moved closer.

"Um, yes. Yes it is."

"And teenagers *are* involved in this violent behavior?"

"Yes, they are," I stammered, trying to summon sarcasm within what used to be shade. "There are definitely teenagers involved in this very, very violent behavior."

The reporter was crafty. "You mean you *agree* that you promote violence?"

Cack to the rescue. He leaned in between us and turned to where the camera would catch his unshaven profile. "Oh yes, ma'am. In fact, you should also include in your report a warning to alert animal rights groups to the fact that innocent earthworms are savagely cut in half by the descending blows of 5-irons swung violently on the golf range owned by the radical capitalistic bigot, Chris Hackett."

She actually took out a pen and scribbled notes. "Was that 5-irons or 6-irons?" she asked without looking up.

"Actually, both," Cack replied and mugged for the camera. "Both a 5-iron and a 6-iron will rip the body of an earthworm clean in half."

Still jotting, she shuddered, perhaps to return the sarcasm.

Cack shifted the golf bag onto his left shoulder and moved closer to the reporter, invading her personal space. In an ultra-serious voice he said into her mic, "Ma'am, I've seen so many decapitated earthworms on golf ranges that I fear the viewings have dulled me to the harshness of death itself."

I pinched my nose to keep from snorting out loud. Sometimes the only way to deal with a manipulator is to play the part of a smart aleck—and the Cackster deserved an Emmy.

Lin and her gallery had gathered around the tenth tee, and most of them were laughing. This should not have surprised me, this so-called *interview* and the attempt at gamesmanship, er, gameswomanship.

Sweaty and disgusted, I remained under the oak and glared at the reporter. "You were hired by Lin? A paid distractor?"

She turned and walked away, her camerawoman right behind her. Under the moss and limbs her reply was weak. "I cannot reveal my employer," she said.

After a pit stop for cold Gatorades, Cack handed me one of the bottles and slumped toward the tenth tee, the bag heavy on his shoulder. He twisted off the cap of his bottle and gulped with a Southern tenacity that I tried to copy but could not.

"C'mon, Chris," he said, "let's go win one for American manhood."

More determined than ever, I strode into the sunlight and eyed the fairway of the tenth hole. At the tee box the pro-Lin spectators parted and let us through. A few giggles lingered around us, and warm whiffs of fertilizer rose from the turf of Yeamans Hall Club.

Before I teed off on the tenth hole, I glanced at Lin and pointed with my club at the tree where the reporter had interviewed me. "Nice try."

Her gaze never left the ground. "I have no idea what you're talking about, Chris."

That was the last thing she said to me for a long while. Her minions, however, were a different story.

For the next hour and a half Cack and I endured taunts, wild speculations about our love lives, and, on three occasions, lipstick tubes flung at my golf ball as I prepared to swing. The worst breech of etiquette occurred in the long grass alongside the fourteenth fairway—after we'd helped Lin look for her ball, Cack returned to my golf bag only to discover that someone had squirted liquid hand soap down the shafts and onto the grips of my clubs.

Retaliation was not an option—no way was I getting into a mudslinging war with all these women. Plus, I had no way of knowing if Lin had ordered such misconduct or if a member of the gallery had acted of her own accord. So Cack and I took the high road. We found a water cooler behind the next green and spent ten minutes cleaning the grips.

"Ridiculous," he muttered and dried the last club with his towel.

To her credit, Lin had avoided hitting into more sand bunkers and made a couple of long putts, which were greeted with mass hysteria, not to mention some manic scoreboard pumping by the scorekeeper. After I holed a twenty-foot putt at the seventeenth—which was greeted with pure silence—the updated scoreboard read:

	#10	#11	#12	#13	#14	#15	#16	#17	#18	Total
The Great Eve:	46	5	4	6	4	5	5	3	4	
Passive Adam:	38	4	5	6	3	6	4	3	3	

So far, Lin had taken a total of 82 strokes, and I had taken 72. Minus her ten shot allowance, we were now tied, with one hole left to play.

Cack hoisted the bag over his shoulder and mumbled something about wishing we would have rented a cart. I could tell he'd grown tired of being in the sun—and being harassed. Together we walked a distance behind the women toward the eighteenth tee.

"Chris," he said between breaths, "I know if you lose this match you have to attend Lin's class, but tell me again what happens if you *win* the bet?"

I pulled a golf glove from my pocket and slipped it onto my left hand. "If I win, I get half the stage time in her class, a chance to share the male perspective on getting along with the opposite sex. And I regain my dignity."

He trudged on a few steps before whispering, "Just how much do you know about getting along with the opposite sex?"

"Not a whole lot really, given my track record. I blurted out the challenge after Lin ticked me off with her antimale comments."

Another few paces—it was a long walk from the seventeenth green to the eighteenth tee—and Cack stopped on the cart path. "Let me get this straight. No matter what happens on this last hole…whether you win or lose, you'll still end up in a class with that caustic woman and her soap-squirting cronies?"

Cack had a way with words, and I could only grin and say, "Never thought about it quite like that, but I suppose that's the gist of it."

He strode ahead and mumbled, "Pitiful bet, just pitiful."

The last hole at Yeamans Hall is a par five of more than 500 yards, long and flat and bisected by a grouping of sand bunkers which cut into the fairway. We arrived at the tee box to boisterous chants of "Yeah woman! Yeah woman!"

Despite the lack of originality—the same chant had burst forth at least thirty times during the match—the enthusiasm and bias never wavered. As had been the case all day, I would play from the blue tees, then Lin would play some forty or fifty yards ahead, from the red tees.

Except when I stepped up to the teeing ground to hit my first shot, I saw no red tees. I just saw a second group of women standing along the cart path on the left side, at least a hundred-fifty yards away.

I hit my tee shot well, a hooking ball that landed in the rough but bounded back into the fairway. Satisfied, I handed my club to Cack, who stood on his toes, his eyebrows raised in concern.

"What's the matter, Cack?"

He pointed in the distance with my club. "The red tees…they're not just fifty yards ahead like the other holes, they're more like a hundred-fifty yards ahead."

That was way too much of a distance advantage for my opponent; she could easily win the hole from up there. "Think her gallery moved the tees up while we were back there talking?" I inquired.

Cack rolled his eyes. "Duh! After they've thrown lipstick tubes at us and filled your golf bag with Dial antibacterial, you think they'd hesitate to move the *tee markers*?"

I cupped my hands over my mouth and yelled ahead. "Lin, did your gallery move the tee markers?"

She had already hit her first shot and was striding down the fairway, her ball some ninety yards ahead of my own.

Ten minutes later I holed a short putt for a 5. She holed her own putt for a score of 4.

Women hugged and women yelled. Women cheered and women clapped. A gnawing, hollow feeling overcame me. Not so much at the score, but at how badly the game had been disrespected.

I was fine with a few natural serpents slithering around a golf course—lizards, gators, even a few moccasins—but this self-absorbed, manipulative type had no place in the sport.

I waited beside the green to speak to Lin, who at the moment was engulfed by her yes-women, reveling in yet another round of "Yeah woman." She broke through her supporters, eyed Cack and me standing on the fringe of the green, and promptly gave us both the briefest of handshakes.

All she said was, "See you Tuesday night in my class."

And all I could reply was, "I'll bring my bulletproof vest."

Now beneath the oak and striding for the parking lot, she spoke over her shoulder. "Wear whatever you like. You can even sit wherever you like. I won't mind if you're not in the front row."

In seconds she and her supporters were gone, and the Yeamans Hall Club returned to its natural state—calm and genteel.

Cack and I spoke little on the drive back to my range, though I managed a smile when I checked my lesson book and saw that Molly was due back the next afternoon.

4

LESSON FOR TODAY

During a round of social golf, especially when the round involves a man and a woman, the man will frequently get distracted and hit an awful tee shot. The wise female (if interested in the male) will then call out, "mulligan," a phrase which allows the man a second chance, an opportunity to begin anew.

*Note: The rules of golf make no mention of mulligans. Allowing a partner to hit a second tee ball is strictly social etiquette.

On the private acre of grass at the end of my driving range, Mrs. Dupree paused from her lesson to offer a snack to her pet. This tiny canine she referred to as her "one-brick dog." She had explained upon arrival her definition of a one-brick dog: this is a dog so tiny that if you tie a few feet of string from its collar to a single brick, it cannot run away. Thus anchored, her pet sat patiently on the grass, tethered to a red brick and nibbling at the corner of a doggie biscuit.

Mrs. Dupree had shown moderate improvement in her golf game, though she lacked power due to an improper weight shift. I stepped back to watch her alignment, knowing that she was trying to hit the 100-yard marker. "Just how well do you know Lin Givens?" I asked between shots.

"Not well," she said and exchanged her 8-iron for a 7. "I only met her once, at a Labor Day party a week ago."

She hit three more shots, and we watched them all slice to the right. Her one-brick dog yelped after each swing, desperate to chase the golf balls.

"Did you not know that she's a radical feminist?"

"Lin?" Mrs. Dupree asked, frowning at yet another slice. "I suppose she can be a bit intense. But if you didn't like her class, you certainly don't have to go back."

Mrs. Dupree then hit two more slices and frowned in disdain as the balls dribbled to a stop on the grass.

I used the grip end of a 5-iron to nudge her feet more in line with the target. "And I suppose you had no idea about the content of her class?"

Frustrated at her slice, Mrs. Dupree plunked her 7-iron back into her bag and drew out a 5-wood. "All I knew was that the class was about understanding the opposite sex. Are you saying it wasn't about that?"

"More like humiliating the opposite sex."

She looked shocked. "Well, like I said, you certainly don't have to go back."

"Yes, I do. I lost a golf bet."

She paused from swatting golf balls and rested her club across her shoulders. "You lost to Lin-the-feminist...at *golf*? You, the great instructor?"

"I gave her too many handicap strokes. Plus, she and her friends cheated."

Mrs. Dupree shook her head in disbelief and returned to her slicing. During the next half hour I did my best to cure her slice, though she did not seem overly interested in improving; apparently, golf lessons were just something to bide her time while her well-connected husband campaigned for state office.

My policy was to avoid political discussions with students, and with a check of my watch I had the perfect excuse. "Mrs. Dupree, I'm afraid I have another lesson to give in two minutes."

She stuffed her 5-wood back into her bag, pulled a towel from a side pocket, and dabbed her forehead "Is she female? Single and cute?"

"How'd you ever guess?"

"I saw her as I was leaving the other day. You looked quite interested, more like a suitor than a teacher."

I faced the sun, hoping it would help hide my blush. "She has potential," I said, "and so does your golf game."

Satisfied with her modest improvement, she left the range with her dog in tow, offering up a promise to return again next week. Golf bag over her shoulder, she departed through the pro shop. I heard her walking across the pea gravel—*crunch, crunch, yelp, ruff ruff*—and I looked back through my chain-link fence and saw her pop the trunk of her Mercedes.

Mrs. Dupree set her golf bag inside along with her single red brick, then she put her featherweight dog in the backseat. She also pulled out a folded T-shirt and waved it at me. She raised her voice across the parking lot, across the fence, and twenty yards of Bermuda. "Chris, if that Lin person really is a feminist and cheats at golf, then you should go to her class in this shirt. It's my husband's, but go ahead and take it. He has three."

From the hitting mats I waved okay, having no idea what she was talking about. "Just leave it there on the fence, Mrs. Dupree. I'll get it shortly."

She flung it across the fence, hurried back to her car, and sped away. My gut told me Mrs. Dupree was a woefully bored member of the wealthy elite, albeit a generous one. As she roared off in her Mercedes, another woman pulled into her vacated parking place.

Molly opened the car door and stood slowly in her white shirt, yellow golf skirt, and matching yellow visor. Yowza.

I hurried to my shop and filled a jumbo-size bucket with golf balls.

"How did the bet go?" asked Molly, already forty minutes into her one-hour lesson.

It was five forty-five, and she had brought for a second time her enthusiasm for learning the proper swing, not to mention her flirtatious manner. "You won, didn't you?" she continued. "You won five hundred bucks from the man-hater and donated it all to something manly like the National Rifle Association?"

On the far left side of my golf range, where I preferred to teach in privacy and away from the crowd, I examined her grip and fielded her questions.

"No, unfortunately I didn't win. But right now let's concentrate on your grip."

Molly also needed to learn to stop lifting her arms as she struck a golf ball, which resulted in a topped shot, the ball dribbling hopelessly in front of the hitting mat and lacking any notion of power or control.

She seemed to enjoy my helping her with her grip, and when she finally wrapped her fingers properly around the club, I decided to give myself permission to get personal. I asked her what she did for a living.

She hit a ball and watched it sail fifty yards in the air. "Go ahead—guess."

"Pharmaceutical sales?" I asked and rolled another ball into position.

"Guess again." She hit a second and a third shot, both pulled left of the target.

"Software sales? Something that requires personality?"

She hit one more. "Not even close. I work in the midst of chaos and try to decipher a phenomenon known as spin."

Her clues were as confusing as her golf swing. "Golf ball sales? They spin a lot, ya know."

She hit another ball and followed its flight—as far right as the previous one had flown left. "I meant *human* spin, Chris. I *analyze* spin. How certain people distort facts and play with the truth."

"Oh no," I said with mock disdain, "you're in politics."

She smiled, hit three more balls off-line. "I'm a political analyst and correspondent, studying demographics and voting patterns in the Deep South. I'm asked to be on TV now and then. I'll be in Charleston for two more weeks."

My questions came fast, as did her answers. Between swings she told me she was a Purdue graduate and a communications major, now living in D.C. After Charleston, she would head to Alabama for a week of work before hurrying back to D.C. to cover a round of debates.

I was disappointed to know that she wasn't a local. And yet, the temporal nature of her visit heightened my sense of urgency to make an impression, to show her a bit of my world. The only thing I could think of, as she finished her lesson and brushed a few grass clippings from her yellow skirt, was to offer her a tour of my facility.

She accepted, and we left her golf bag leaning against the pro shop and walked around behind the hitting mats, where some twenty customers flailed away. The after-work crowd had drifted in—range rats in obligatory golf duds, corporate folk in business casual, teenagers in whatever. Near the end of the range a young father instructed his toddler how to grip the club, and I felt a tinge of envy, what with my unfulfilled desire to have a son of my own.

"Do you give teenagers a discount?" Molly asked, watching youthful golfers swing youthfully.

"Um, not very often...but that's a great idea." My attempt to be agreeable.

Though she had little talent for the game, Molly seemed a degree more polished than my other female students. I couldn't help but notice her quick wit, perfect posture, and TV-babe haircut. We strolled toward the setting sun, and squinting I explained to her how I'd begun with just ten mats, adding more as the business grew, until now I was maxed out at thirty-six mats while still leaving a natural grass area for tournament players and low-handicappers.

"A little something for everyone?" she asked in midstride. "Sounds like some congressmen I know."

Past the last mat on the right—I had noted that 27 of the 36 were occupied, always a good percentage—I showed her the Groundskeeper Café. Then, behind Cack's table, the maintenance shed. Its automatic garage door was open, and Molly surprised me by pointing inside. "Can we take a look?"

I had no idea why this classy woman wanted to see the maintenance shed, but I strolled in with her and promptly discovered the object of her curiosity—she'd spotted Cack's customized golf cart, with the metal cage shaped like a top hat.

"What exactly is *that* thing?" she asked, pointing at the steel mesh rising over the seat and steering wheel.

"It's our Taunt-mobile. My groundskeeper, whom you met in the pro shop, drives it around on Wednesday nights and incites the customers through a bullhorn. People get all worked up and try to hit him. It's great for business."

Molly put a finger to her lips. She appeared deep in thought. "He *incites* them? How does he do that?"

I propped one foot on the cart's front bumper. "Mostly he drives around in figure eights and tells people they stink at golf. He's got some pretty good one-liners."

She motioned to the driver's door and raised an eyebrow. "May I?"

"Sit in it?"

She nodded. "Just for a minute."

Not questioning her motives, I opened the caged door and helped her inside. She sat behind the wheel and ran her hands across the steering wheel. Then she looked on the seat beside her and noted the bullhorn that Cack had left there. Through half-inch mesh she looked up at me. "Chris, have you ever thought about having your buddy shout *political* insults through this caged thingamajig?"

"Um, no. Never entered my mind."

Molly pulled the caged door till it clanked shut. "Then perhaps it's time to experiment, mister." Still on the outside looking in, I was hoping she would not do what she did.

She turned the key and started the cart.

"You really shouldn't," I said, one hand holding the steel cage. "You might not get the response you're hoping for."

She picked up the bullhorn, pointed it at me, and put her lips to the mouthpiece. Then, in the voice of a carnival barker, "I guess ya never know till you try."

She pressed the gas and took off out of the maintenance shed and drove into the middle of my range. Stunned at her boldness and initiative, I scrambled out of the shed and up a small rise before pausing behind the last mat to watch my customers react.

At first nothing happened. Customers continued with their practice and in general acted like Molly was just out there to pick up golf balls.

But then, in the midst of a long turn away from the sun, she pulled the bullhorn to her lips and uttered words that made me cringe. "Okay, all you Carolina hackers, I'm pro-Democrat, pro-choice, anti-Bush, and antiwar! And if you don't like it…just try to hit me!"

Then she blazed across the Bermuda, turning in circles around the 100-yard and 150-yard markers.

Golf balls flew at her as if shot from Gatling guns.

Two businessmen stripped off their ties and swung with the kind of ferocity that only testosterone can yield. Women muttered, "The audacity of her!" and fired away.

One redneckish range rat shouted, "Them's fightin' words," teed up three balls in a row, and hit them as fast as he could swing.

This was not the playful mock anger directed at Cack on Wednesday nights; this was deep-seated and personal. And perhaps very good for business.

When Molly repeated her charge, adding a line about, "Conservatives swing like uncoordinated Bible-thumpers," customers sprinted to the pro shop to buy more buckets of balls.

"Who is that nutcase out there?" a guy asked as he passed me with two buckets.

I could only shrug. I was tempted to chase her out across the range, though fear of being struck by a multitude of golf balls kept me planted. Plus she drove like a crazy woman.

Cack, in something resembling a jealous fit, came running out of the pro shop in his overalls. He hurried behind the hitting mats, on a beeline for his boss.

"Who took my job?" he demanded. He breathed heavily and pointed at Molly. "I'm the only one who gets to antagonize the customers."

I watched her circle the range, white pellets bouncing around the cart. "She's just experimenting a bit, Cack. She's in politics…and came up with a new idea."

Neither his posture nor his tone could hide his jealousy. "But we only do this on Wednesday nights. Six forty-four, remember? I have flyers posted all over."

"I know, buddy. But her idea just might—"

She had the bullhorn to her lips again.

We watched this free spirit incite the crowd, provoking strenuous swings and mass determination; everyone on the range was firing away at her. Then Molly shouted, "Warmongers make terrrrrible golfers."

My groundskeeper looked on in astonishment. "Wish I'd thought of that one," he muttered. "Does this mean I'm demoted?"

"No, but I think the two of you should have a powwow and come up with more ways to milk the polarization of the country."

Cack frowned. "Here you go with those big words again." He looked like he wanted to say something else, something like, "'Do I get to drive the cart more than she does?" but instead he turned and hurried back to the pro shop to sell buckets of golf balls to our right-leaning customers.

Ten minutes later Molly returned to the maintenance shed, no dents evident in either the cart or herself. "The experiment worked," she said and wiped the sweat from her eyes. I opened the caged door and helped her out, thinking that I should have been mad. But somehow that emotion was unavailable—she had a kind of mischievous glow about her.

No golf student had ever pulled a stunt like that, and I was at a loss what to say to her, caught as I was between attraction and surprise. All I managed at first was, "Are you really so anticonservative?"

She brushed some grass clippings from her shorts and shook her head. "No, not at all. And I'm not pro-choice either. I just figured since this is South Carolina, I'd try to stir some people up and help you sell golf balls."

Behind us I heard customers shouting, "Bring her out again!"

"Should I go back out?" Molly inquired, peeking out the door of the maintenance shed. "They really seem to hate me."

I peeked around her. "Yes...they do."

She did not give an encore—I wouldn't let her—but instead asked to see the rest of the equipment we used to maintain the business. I concurred, well aware that, if interested, a female will show curiosity about a man's vocation.

After I showed her the tumbler—a machine which washed thousands of dirty golf balls each night—we left the shed and strolled back uphill toward the pro shop. My customers too had returned to normalcy; they looked almost bored now, firing away at stationary targets.

Molly retrieved her golf bag from the bag stand, and we backed up into the shade of an awning that protruded from the rear of my pro shop. "Chris," she said, motioning to the golf range, "I know a candidate who's looking for unique ways to interact with the public. How would you feel if I encouraged him to stop by here and hit golf balls at a caricature of his opponent?"

"Namely Cack?"

"Could be great for business during the political season."

Dollar signs and enraged hackers competed for brain space. "Would this mean free advertising?"

"Without a doubt." She pulled a club from her bag and practiced her grip.

"That candidate isn't named Lin, is she?"

"No, *his* name is Bill."

I twitched my lip left and right, wondering what I might be getting into. "But I want my golf range to be an inclusive kind of place, not associated with one political stance or another."

She smiled and nodded as if expecting my answer. "What if you offered something like a Friday night special for conservatives, followed by a Saturday night special for liberals? That would brand you as both a fun and inclusive kind of entrepreneur."

Election year advertising slogans orbited in my head. *Whack the Democrat? Followed up the next night with Whack the Republican?*

The daze that enveloped me continued until she poked my rib with her 5-iron. "Chris, it was just a thought…but this could have *awesome* possibilities."

I thought of Cack and his love of riling the customers. "You'll share your insults with my groundskeeper?"

"Glad to. Just tell Cack to have his bullhorn ready."

I wanted to ask Molly if she wanted to go grab some dinner, but I glanced at my watch and saw 7:43. I had never reneged on a bet in my life, and I cringed at the realization that tonight was a Tuesday.

With her golf bag over her shoulder, Molly pulled open the back door to my pro shop and moved toward the front exit.

I hurried past her and opened the front door for her. "Can I get your cell number?" I asked. "Maybe call you one day soon?"

She stopped in the pea gravel, smiled with a hint of embarrassment, and wrote her number on the back of a business card.

She handed me the card, and then with one brief wave she was gone.

This new Eve intrigued me; she seemed quite witty, a bit sassy, and goofily spontaneous. But then there was that other one, the one who called herself *The Great Eve,* and I had to go listen to another of her man-blaming manifestos.

5

LESSON FOR TODAY

When leading a match (or debating an issue),
an overconfident opponent will often relax and
make a critical error in judgment. The intelligent
player will then seize this opportunity and play
aggressively.

In Conference Room #4 at the Hyatt, I sat in the back row again, wearing the T-shirt that Mrs. Dupree had left hanging atop the chain-link fence. The words screen-printed on the front of my shirt were red and bold and vivid and, at least within my present company, controversial. *Rush Limbaugh Rocks!*

I felt silly in the shirt, since I rarely listened to talk radio. Still, it was the best way I knew to get back at the women who had poured hand soap on my golf grips, moved the tee markers forward, and taunted me during my backswing.

"Ladies, there is one thing about man that we know to be true." From the stage Lin scanned the gathering, most of whom nodded in agreement with her every word. "Who can finish this sentence? Manhood is in a state of . . . ?"

A third row yes-woman raised her hand. "A state of denial?"

"Close, but not quite."

Cecelia stood and said, "I know the answer. Manhood is in a state of *confusion!*"

Lin thrust a fist into the air. "Bingo," she gushed. "And can you tell us why?"

Cecilia turned to face the rows behind her. "Yep, I know manhood is in a state of confusion 'cause my ex-boyfriend was just that—very, very confused. He was confused over whether he should keep a job, confused if he was allowed to date other women after he asked me to go steady, and confused why I broke us up."

Howls of laughter.

Lin looked quite pleased. "Manhood has been in a state of confusion for thousands of years," she said, "all because Adam did not learn from Eve as she asserted her great power and independence."

Applause, whoops, whistles.

I shook my head, wanting to bolt but aware that I had lost a bet. At least technically.

Lin then reached inside her podium and drew out a thick stack of white computer paper. "Ladies, in order to bond with each other, I think we should share the experiences we've endured with uncommunicative and misguided members of the opposite sex." She handed the blank paper to a woman in the front row and asked her to give everyone four sheets.

Lin then returned to her mic and grasped it with both hands. "This is an in-class assignment: to write a paper on how the opposite sex has disappointed you. You do this, too, Chris," she said. "It'll be good for you...and also for that hate-monger you're advertising on your T-shirt."

Her instructions lingered over the eight rows of occupied chairs and did so with a kind of oratorical stench. Discrimination has a distinct odor.

I did not want to write about disappointment. I wanted to write about hope. But since there was currently one female who had definitely disappointed me—Lin herself—I decided to include her in my paper, a paper centered in my favorite sport.

And so I wrote. For the entire fifty minutes we had left in class, I never stopped moving my black ink pen across the page. The story came drifting in out of the ether, in clumps of bold vision it drifted—and my only goal was for the words to keep up with the film scrolling inside my head.

The Day That Money Ruined Golf
(but gained me a wife)
by Christopher Hackett

It began, of course, on eBay. Someone listed for sale a golf club (a 47" driver), boasting that it was "sliceless, hook-less, and powered a golf ball 400 yards, dead straight, every time, no matter who swung the club."

The club was called a Super Blaster, and the ad turned out to be true.

Within a month, the seller sold four million Super Blasters at a cost of eight hundred dollars each. Of course, this being eBay, someone bought a dozen, relisted them as Super-Duper Blasters, and sold them for a thousand dollars each. But that is just a capitalistic footnote to the story.

Golfers all across America loved their Super Blasters. Some loved them so much they bought specially designed golf luggage to protect their expensive club en route to a golf course. But course owners around the world were not pleased at all over the arrival of Super Blasters, including owners in Scotland, long considered the home of golf.

"Bring back the dignity of the grand game!" they shouted in deep Scottish brogues.

In the United States, golf course owners from Winged Foot to Pebble Beach to Augusta National complained that their once mighty courses were now a pushover for any grandma or kindergartener who wielded a Super Blaster. The owners talked among themselves, criticizing the manufacturer of the Super Blaster and wondering how to once again make their courses longer and more challenging. They needed more land. But real estate—oh, the skyrocketing prices!—prevented the owners from buying more. This was because it was now common knowledge among neighbors that the golf courses were a pushover and that management needed to acquire more property in order to lengthen the courses. So, no one would sell. The price of a 3,000 square foot home behind the fifth tee at Winged Foot went from 4 million dollars to 14 million overnight. Prices at Pebble Beach were three times that.

"But that's outrageous!" cried the golf course owners, waving Want to Buy contracts in the faces of property owners. "We don't have that kind of money to throw around."

"We know," said the neighbors, "but we now own Super Blasters ourselves and will continue to shoot record low scores on your once-heralded golf course."

Each time a course owner knocked on a homeowner's door, someone came to the door brandishing a brand new Super Blaster, a tactic which infuriated the golf course owners to the eighteenth degree.

The official rules committee of golf, the USGA—who had approved the Super Blaster for use—were of no help at all to the course owners. This was because the manufacturer of the Super Blaster had delivered suitcases of cash to each member of the USGA rules committee, a bribe of monumental consequences.

What no one knew—there was much speculation on this matter—was who was behind the manufacture and sale of this golf-ruining new product. Was the Super Blaster conceived by a brilliant Chinese inventor in Beijing? Was it a consortium of European business leaders? Or perhaps a sports-minded Jamaican who, while smoking something entirely illegal, had dreamed up the Super Blaster beneath a palm tree? Surely it wasn't Nike! Or TaylorMade. Or PING or any other top golf company. No, it was none of them. In fact, none of the golf companies had a product to compete with the Super Blaster, and so these companies began losing out big time—losing sales, customers, even employees.

Especially female employees.

The manufacturer of the Super Blaster turned out to be The Progressive Golf Company, based in Charleston, South Carolina, which was owned and operated by Lin Givens. Lin was a radical women's rights leader, public speaker, man-hater, and fairly good golfer herself (though sometimes she cheated).

Lin had hired top scientists from all over the planet—all of them females—to design and build a product that would make the sport of golf so easy, so absolutely boring, that men would quit the game, resign from male-dominated country clubs, and allow her and her rich female friends to take over. Lin even formed a sales company that she called the Super Blaster Corporation.

Millions of women from across the country were enticed to join the Super Blaster Corporation as independent sales reps, much like Mary Kay salespeople, although Lin would never give a pink Cadillac to anyone, because in her view the color pink was sexist. So she promised successful saleswomen a navy blue Hummer with front license plates that read "EVE RULES!"

One of the few women in Charleston who did not sign up to sell Super Blasters was a slender, thirtyish gal, single and with a big smile, who showed up at Hack's Golf Learning Center on a Wednesday night during Happy Hour when large buckets of balls were two for the price of one. She spotted a sign propped up on the driving range fence: NO SUPER BLASTERS ALLOWED AT THIS GOLF RANGE! This was because the handsome young owner's fence only extended 315 yards, thus any club that would propel a golf ball 400 yards in the air would inevitably send all the range balls over the fence and out into the woods, causing no shortage of growls and complaints from the eccentric old groundskeeper, Cack, whose name just happened to rhyme with Hack.

"Why," asked the beautiful single woman, "don't you allow Super Blasters here?"

"Because they are killing the sport of golf!" the handsome young owner replied, rubbing sunblock with an SPF of 40 on his muscular arms.

The beautiful young woman came closer and flashed a friendly smile. "Ya know, I agree with you."

Suspicious, the handsome owner replied, "Don't you own a Super Blaster, ma'am? All women have one now."

"Oh, surely *not*!" she replied. "I would never own one. In fact, I hate Super Blasters. They've put my father's golf course out of business. It's made the sport too easy, and now everyone shoots a low score and quits the game out of sheer boredom."

The handsome young owner moved closer. "My thoughts exactly, Miss…Miss…I'm sorry, I didn't get your name."

"Molly," she said, extending her hand. "Molly Cusack."

"Did you say 'Cusack'?"

"Yes, I said 'Cusack.'"

The handsome young owner smiled, as he knew that such a poetic name must be fate. *At a range called Hack's, on the night of Whack the Cack, I meet Molly Cusack, and I should never turn back…to look at any other woman…ever again.*

His quickly conjured rhyme made the handsome young owner smile.

"What do you do for a living, Molly?" he asked her.

"I'm in advertising, in charge of national ads for an Internet company."

"So, you can impact what people think about a particular product?"

"I do it all the time," she said and pulled her Nike 3-wood from her golf bag. She teed a ball and took a practice swing. "Why? You want to advertise something?"

The handsome young owner put a finger to his lips, said, "Shhh," and motioned for her to huddle with him to discuss a new ad.

During the next half hour, at the private end of the driving range, the handsome young owner and the beautiful young Molly came up with a plan—a plan to restore dignity to the grand game of golf.

The next day, on every TV network and nationally syndicated radio show, the facts hit the proverbial media fan: Super Blasters contain plutonium alloy compounds, which cause cancer of the hands and make your fingers rot off!

The following day 3 million, nine hundred and ninety-eight thousand Super Blasters went on sale on eBay from a nickel to three dollars and forty-five cents. No one would bid, though, even when prices dropped to two cents each.

The day after the news ran on TV and everywhere else, the handsome young range owner asked Molly for a date. At an outdoor café they shared a pepperoni pizza. Molly ate three slices. He ate five.

The handsome young range owner married Molly the following summer, a June wedding on the eighteenth green at Pebble Beach, where they were given a lifetime membership for saving the grand game of golf. They honeymooned on a sailboat in the Fiji Islands. Cack was the best man.

Lin Givens was forced by the government to refund all monies to former Super Blaster owners. She declared bankruptcy and was convicted of fraud and reckless endangerment of golfers. She was banished to Siberia, where even today she is forced to make snow cones for eighty hours a week and serve them from a wooden shack to cute little Siberian children. Every day Lin sits by herself in that cold, cold shack and pours the same pink syrup over crushed ice and makes pink snow cones, the very color that she loathes. The cute little Siberian kids wonder why she never smiles.

The end.

"Has everyone completed their papers?" Lin asked the class. "Hurry please, ladies. Only two minutes left. Next week I'm going to read these back."

I passed mine into the growing pile and muttered, "Finished."

6

LESSON FOR TODAY

When competing in a team event (or when getting to know a new love interest), it is usually wise to allow your partner to play to his or her strengths. This strategy can reap unimagined benefits for the lesser-skilled partner.

At closing time on Thursday, Cack and I gathered on opposite sides of the counter and checked off items from our nightly to-do list: Equipment cleaned and prepared for the next day. Carts filled with gas. Range balls picked up and fed into the washer. Automatic sprinklers set for night watering. Grass seed spread over fresh divots.

Today had been slow, and now I toiled over a half-empty register, counting bills while Cack counted the coins.

"Too many kids paying with nickels and dimes," he muttered. "We should figure out a way to solicit wealthy folk."

After stuffing the money into deposit envelopes, we hung around the shop and talked about the grass wilting in the left corner of the range and what could be done about it. Cack said his solution depended on the weather, so he turned on our TV mounted on the wall behind the cash register.

The ten o'clock news blared, filled with crime sensational-ized, sports overdramatized, and politics politicized. After the weather report—low 80's and sunny for the balance of Sep-tember was the weather girl's giggly estimate—Cack grabbed a Mountain Dew from our fridge and said he was done for the night.

"Be thinking about that sickly Bermuda," I said.

At the front door he raised his drink can in acknowledg-ment. Or perhaps the gesture was his toast to another day well lived. You never knew with Cack. Without further communica-tion he pushed open the glass door and departed.

I looked up from my labors to see the TV anchorman welcome a guest to his news desk. It was Molly, easing into a chair on the studio set. She sported the kind of light blue outfit that flatters ninety-percent of the population, especially those on television. She looked prepared, professional, and ready to engage.

The anchor—a man whose hair looked glued on and who went by the name of Dirk Denmark—introduced her and asked if any new trends had emerged in the election battles. The ques-tion sounded loaded, though I had no idea just how loaded, or in which direction the political pistol might be aimed.

Molly flirted with the camera and said, "Thank you, Dirk. It seems in this election year, the economic division of America has become a huge issue. Higher wage earners benefit more from across-the-board wage hikes, and of course real estate prices bolster the upper class even more. And who can afford ten dollar movie tickets every weekend for a family of four?"

This didn't sound like any new trend to me.

Dirk Denmark interrupted my thoughts. "It seems, Molly, that not only has housing and entertainment turned a cold shoulder to the common man and the disadvantaged, but cer-tain segments of the sports world have followed suit."

Please mention golf. Please please please!

Molly took the bait and ran with it. "Right again, Dirk. And the sport that embodies this division the most is golf, traditionally the sport of the rich. Nowhere would a policy of inclusion resonate like it would if people of all races, creeds, and social status were encouraged to participate at a golf course."

Dirk's next line was an even juicier form of bait. "And have you discovered a course or a country club in the Charleston area that actively supports such inclusion?"

Molly adjusted the mic on her lapel. "Perhaps not 'actively.' But one enterprising Charleston golf range owner has figured out a way to profit from the divisive and sometimes angry nature of American political discourse. He encourages folks from either side, whether conservative or liberal, to come out and whop golf balls at their taunting opposition, who insult them from inside a caged golf cart."

Love the phrase "taunting opposition," Molly, but please mention Hacks!

Dirk Denmark feigned shock. "Molly, are you saying that political opponents can actually hit golf balls at each other?"

Molly smiled into the camera and said, "Correct, Dirk. And the entrepreneur behind this new craze is one Chris Hackett, owner of Hack's Golf Learning Center, who gave me a golf lesson yesterday afternoon. His plan is to open his range this Friday evening at six o'clock for all conservatives who wish to 'Whop a Liberal.'"

It's "whack" a liberal, Molly, not whop.

In a kind of mock surprise—this whole thing was so staged that it sounded quite cheesy, as if the station needed to fill two minutes of airtime on a slow night—Dirk Denmark's jaw descended to his lap. And when finally he raised his jaw back to its original position, he managed to ask, "Is there a reciprocal evening planned for our left-leaning viewers?"

Molly nodded with courtesy and professionalism. "Why of course, Dirk. Glad you asked. Saturday night Chris invites all who lean left to bring their clubs—or borrow some of his own—for a round of 'Whop the Conservative.' Range balls are said to be priced as low as anywhere in the county."

A photo of my golf range, then one of Cack's custom cart, showed on the TV screen.

Yes!

When the photos disappeared and the live studio set shown again, Dirk Denmark was patting his hair into place. He recovered quickly. "And what, Molly, would this range owner say to the independents and libertarians in our viewing audience?"

She never flinched. "They're invited to swing away on either night. Chris Hackett claims he has no prejudices, just thousands of golf balls at the ready."

"No spin?" asked Dirk.

"Oh yes, the golf balls at Hack's spin in either direction."

"They curve both left and right, eh?" Corny laughter from Dirk Denmark.

Molly rolled her eyes and said, "You got it, Dirk."

The publicity was overwhelming. Seemed half of Charleston's Republican Party showed up Friday night, including candidates for the State House of Representatives, local Sheriff, and County Council.

Cack, wary and pessimistic, told me early that afternoon in the shed that getting involved in any kind of politics was a bad move. "Too much hysteria," he said, helping me load plastic buckets with fresh-washed golf balls. "On both sides of the aisle."

Nevertheless, by 5:30 p.m. campaign signs stood quivering in the grass around my property. Volunteers even handed out flyers as customers walked across the pea gravel. I imagined the customer's surprise when they approached my golf shop— *crunch, crunch, "Vote for Bill!"*

For a moment I even considered changing my sign out front from HACK'S to POLITICAL HACK'S: Our Golf Balls Curve Both Ways!

Then there were the cameras. Political aides brought cameras of many makes, and flashes flashed as candidates took wild swings at independent golf balls.

Conservatives of all shapes and sizes occupied the thirty-six hitting mats and the natural turf. The people were loose, wired, ready for battle. I could not recall a single instance in my six years of owning the range where all the mats were full. Golf was a sport whose participation numbers had not grown at all in the past ten years. Despite the promotions and the space-age technology, the game still fought its image of being too difficult and/or too expensive.

But tonight was not about degree of difficulty, nor was it about cost; this was a kind of physical release. Political tensions expressed athletically…or *non-athletically,* if you could have seen the candidates swing. The guy running for State House looked like he was trying to smash rats in a phone booth.

All this even before the taunting began.

A horn honked from the maintenance shed, and Cack zoomed out onto the range. He had installed the horn that morning; he was always tinkering with his caged contraption. He'd even talked of installing chrome wheels, a 10-disk CD changer, and four speakers—a vision he referred to as "Pimp My Golf Cart."

Through the wire mesh, all you could see was an Uncle Sam hat and the bullhorn he held to his lips. He wasted no time. "If you oil barons didn't spend so much on defense, poor kids could play this game too!"

A mild beginning, sure, but enough put-down that golf balls flew in forty directions. *Thwack. Duff. Whiff. Shank. Thud.*

I wondered why Molly had not shown up yet, though I was too busy selling buckets of balls to give it much thought—or to pick up the phone and call her.

People who had never swung a golf club had come to take swats. And if they couldn't hit the ball with their club, or were waiting in line at a mat, they mimicked the teenage girls and threw the balls overhand.

Then Cack got a bit crazy. Somewhere past the 150-yard marker, he stopped his cart, got out, and climbed on top of the steel cage. Light from tall poles illuminated him, and the customers gasped at this daring man in blue overalls. But with his Uncle Sam hat teetering on his head, Cack raised the bullhorn and shouted, "You Republicans couldn't hit the Watergate Hotel if you teed up your golf balls on its front sidewalk!"

He ducked back inside the cart and took off.

Something odd struck me as I watched members of the right flail away, trying to gong the loudmouth. Amongst the eighty or ninety folks spread across the hitting mats and taking turns, the candidates were the ones who took the most time between swings, as if their minds were clogged with political mush. From my perch at the pro shop window I watched them and tried to imagine media-savvy Molly giving them advice:

If you can get on TV at this golf range, and then utter a funny line about how your opponent on the left is so soft on crime that he'd build golf ranges for captured terrorists, you might sway the electorate.

While I was lost in speculation, a conservative teenage girl—who did not dress conservatively—ran into the pro shop. "Chris, please come show us how to hit the cart! My friends and I are terrible at golf!"

I followed her out to the twenty-first mat, where four of her friends were taking turns making awful swings, some throwing the balls harmlessly at Cack's weaving Taunt-mobile.

"No charge for the lesson?" the blond girl asked, while the rest of us watched her miss the ball twice.

"Nope. No charge at all."

With one of their clubs in hand I stepped up on the mat and explained how to hit golf balls at a moving cart. I told them that everyone makes the same mistake: they hit one ball, then reach out with the club to rake the next ball into position, and by the time they aim and strike it, the cart is out of range or has moved so far in the other direction that the shot has no chance.

In midlesson Cack came swooping around the 100-yard marker and said through his bullhorn, "The owner of this range is more crooked than Nixon!"

I ignored the insult as teenagers gathered around me. I told them the way to hit a moving cart with a golf ball is simple: You place five balls in a row on the mat and aim a few yards in front of the cart. Then you hit firmly down on the ball, move quickly to the second ball, and do the same. Then to the third and fourth and fifth. Rapid fire.

"Remember, girls," I said in my most instructive voice, "you are the machine gun; the golf balls are your bullets."

From behind the mat one of the girls said, "Show us, Chris!"

"Nah, I really shouldn't."

All together they blurted, "Pleeease!"

"Well...okay."

I waited for Cack to come circling by again.

He repeated his insult. I obeyed my own instruction and hit the balls quickly. Like white tracer bullets they flew into the night.

Thwack...wide left.

Thwack...wide right.

Thwack...too high.

Thwack...*Clang.* Got him in the front bumper.

Cheers, backslaps, and high fives from teenage girls.

I am young again. I am popular. I am Superman.

Lesson over, I gave the girls their club back and bowed deeply. The blond set seven balls on the mat and whiffed the first three. Cack shouted that she couldn't hit dust bunnies with a broom.

I turned from the chaos to check on my pro shop. Underneath the awning stood a woman more my age. I had wondered why Molly had not arrived with the campaign, though I supposed with her being an analyst and not a local, she wasn't going to show any bias. Still, she alone was the reason for my very crowded and boisterous golf range.

"Is that your girlfriend?" asked one of the teenagers as I departed.

"Just work on your golf swing, miss," I said over my shoulder. They giggled as I hurried back toward my shop.

In jeans and a bright blue *Pro-Dem* T-shirt, Molly looked glad to see me. But after my initial "hello there," she only said, "Great to see you, Chris. But right now I gotta go take my turn in the cart. Cack said it was okay. Wanna grab a pizza later?"

I blurted, "You bet," as she went running down the hill toward the maintenance shed.

Cack met her there, handed off the bullhorn, and secured her inside the cart. He gave her a push start, then paused on the grass and wiped the sweat from his forehead. The night had turned humid, and the right-wingers were yelling for more.

Molly came tearing out from the right side of the range, weaving back and forth to draw attention to herself. In a kind of rolling ad lib she chastened the customers and wasted no time in making the insults personal. She turned the cart around the 100-yard marker and came speeding past the three candidates, all of them male and taking aim.

Then she raised the bullhorn and said, "The libs have prettier wives, and they got them without the benefit of unfair tax cuts for the wealthy!"

The guy running for State House swung so hard he fell down on the mat.

The ball sliced horribly off line, and Molly never missed a beat. She stopped in the middle of the range and shouted, "Slipped on your fat wallet, eh? That happens a lot to you capitalist extremists."

Aides sprinted to my pro shop to buy more buckets of balls.

I sold them plenty, then returned to the window to watch the fireworks. And into the middle of it all, in patriotic red, white, and blue, strode Mrs. Dupree, trolling the range with her one-brick dog and handing out invitations to a party. Hack's had become a nuthouse.

Just when I thought the revelry had peaked, my office phone began ringing. And ringing. One guy who had seen the news bit called in from out of town, wanting me to open "Hack's of Myrtle Beach." Another guy from Los Angeles who was vacationing on Kiawah Island and owned a public course and golf range in LA, requested an instruction manual on how to build a caged cart in the shape of a top hat. Then he asked for a list of Cack's best political one-liners.

I felt the need to protect my eccentric friend, so I told a little Caucasian lie. "Um, sir, Cack is working the range at the moment, infuriating conservatives."

"What about the instruction manual to build the cart cage that looks like a top hat?"

"I don't think there is a manual, sir. Cack freewheeled it. Just him and his welding tool."

The guy paused a moment. "Think he'd build one for me? I'd pay good money."

"I'll ask him when he gets through infuriating the conservatives."

Cack was not overly thrilled by all this attention. Thirty minutes later, while Molly took her second turn at golfer harassment, he burst into the pro shop and told me this stuff could get out of hand, that our once fun-natured little business might become too much of a conduit for competing agendas.

"People are gonna take this too seriously, Chris," he said while staring at the growing pile of cash in our register. "Someone could get hurt."

No one got hurt. And no one budged Cack from his independent ideology. Even better, by the time the customers had left and the lights were turned out on the range, we'd sold fourteen hundred dollars worth of golf balls.

Molly remained in the pro shop with us while I bagged the money and Cack filled out a deposit slip. She gulped from a water bottle before leaning over the counter to watch our progress. With a kind of flirty curiosity she said, "Looks like a good night."

I took a couple of twenties and stuffed them into my shirt pocket. "Pizza money," I said.

I locked up the shop and followed the two of them into the parking lot. There I handed Cack three hundred bucks in cash and told him it was his bonus for "political insults above and beyond the call of duty."

Cack stared at the wad of bills in his hands for a long moment. Then he stuffed the cash into his pocket and said he had no more reservations about the direction of the business.

He and Molly exchanged "nice to meet ya's," and he left whistling. At the door of his pickup he muttered something about the great one-liners he'd dreamed up for Saturday night, when the Democrats would invade us and have their turn on the mats.

At a table for two inside a pizza joint called Andolini's, Molly lowered her menu and said, "You're quite generous with your employees."

I nodded with all the humility I could muster. "Cack is more like a partner than an employee. Besides, the whole insult-the-customers thing was his idea."

Her face went blank. "You mean you didn't think of it yourself?"

"Nope. My insult skills are quite pitiful."

She hid again behind her menu. "Gosh, then I have no reason to be on a dinner date with you."

Before I knew how to respond, she lowered the menu a second time and said, "Just kidding."

"Somehow I expect a lot of that."

After a minute of silence, Molly peered again over her menu. "Chris, do you like banana peppers on your pizza?"

"Yes," I said, studying the list of ingredients, "but only if the peppers invite their cousins, the pepperonis."

She rolled her eyes as if that was the corniest line she'd ever heard. But then Molly smiled and said, "Maybe the pepperonis should invite the black olives."

"And the black olives should insist that the—"

A waitress came by and interrupted our silly first-date banter. But then we began again, and the waitress stood frowning as we debated our way to a seven-topping pizza. The only ingredient blackballed were the anchovies.

By the time only three slices remained on the platter, we had shared the shallower side of first-date basics: her family in New York and Virginia; mine in Georgia and Alabama. She had an older sister; I had an older brother. She liked dalmatians and Siamese cats; I liked labs and absentee cats. She'd seen Irish countrysides and wanted to visit Mexico. I'd seen Mexico and wanted to golf the Irish countryside.

During a lull in the mutual sharing, she picked at the crust of a pizza slice and said, "Chris, there's another reason why I wanted to have a chat tonight."

For a moment she just let the comment hover over the table.

All I could think was, *Here it comes, her next great idea for expanding the customer base at Hack's.*

And for once in my life, I correctly predicted the actions of a female. After she'd eaten the crust—she seemed to like the plain outer crust even more than the ingredients—she dabbed at her mouth with a napkin and set the napkin in her lap. "I need to explain something."

I sought refuge in a long slurp of sweet tea. "You're gonna tell me that the feminists really *did* invent the Super Blaster?"

Molly plucked a lone banana pepper from her plate but stopped short of biting into it. "What are you talking about?"

My pizza slice needed more Parmesan, and I was happy to oblige it. "Never mind. Go ahead and explain what you were going to explain."

She tucked her napkin back into her lap. "You have a good thing going at your golf range, but tonight was just a general bashing of a political ideology. What if you promoted a night where actual opponents—say a local Dem State House candidate against a local Republican State House candidate—both showed up with their fan bases? Then do the same with the mayoral candidates and so forth?"

"I'll give that some thought." A longer gulp of sweet tea helped me process the fact that I needed to shift control of this chat. Moreover, just when I thought we might talk about more personal goals—like what we're looking for in a spouse, if each wanted kids—she remained planted on her favorite subject. Perhaps she was just a bit nervous, this being a first date. Our talk, however, had shifted firmly from pepperoni to politics, a detour that created the conversational lull from which we needed recovery.

I simply blurted it out. "So, do you want kids, Molly?"

Slight hesitation. "With you, or in general?"

"The second one."

She looked confused. "The second *kid*?"

"No, I meant do you want kids in general? I realize that we don't know each other all that well yet, but right now I'm sorta picturing you as the career type who, at age thirty, thinks of parenthood in vague terms of *someday,* a woman who is great at her job but one who just might wake up at age thirty-eight wondering if it is too late for kids. So if this is how you're viewing life, I need to know because someday I'm picturing a crib or two behind the desk of my golf shop and little plastic golf clubs in a rainbow of colors." I paused for a quick breath. "Do you ever think those kind of thoughts?…I mean in *general,* not necessarily with me, or with plastic clubs."

Perhaps this detour was a bit too swift, an unexpected squeal of the relational front tires. But it did serve to stun Molly out of political mode and force on her a kind of wide-eyed, open-mouthed wonder, as if she had never been asked such questions with such boldness—especially on a first date.

"Wow, Chris. You don't waste any time, do you?"

I leaned forward in the booth, eyed her over the napkin holder. "So…do you ever think those kinds of thoughts?"

After several anxious glances around the restaurant, she managed a subdued, "Perhaps. But would you mind if we waited a few more dates before discussing these things in depth?"

This seemed reasonable enough. "Sure," I said and reached for the dinner check.

Our date began its conclusion when Molly explained that she had to be up early for another TV spot, and it ended fully with a gentle handshake at the door of her rental car. I liked her a lot, though I wondered if I'd been too blunt.

"It was nice to chat with you, Chris," she said and let go of my hand. "Although somehow the word 'chat' doesn't feel substantial enough. Let me think on your questions some more…and, um, remember what I suggested about your business."

"Sure. I'll call you in two days."

After I'd closed her door and she'd driven away, I stood there in the empty street for a moment and reconsidered my rather intrusive get-to-know-ya technique. I figured not only did I need to soften my method, but also I should somehow label it, in case I ever needed to share it with a fellow single.

I labeled it THUMPE—The Hackett Unbridled Method of Prospect Evaluation.

Part one was simple: *If you don't want kids, I probably don't want to date you.*

Perhaps Molly had her own methodology, though I wouldn't hazard a guess. A college buddy had told me once that the evaluation systems of women were as varied as the universe of golf swings—and that any man who tried to predict a woman's system was headed for yet another relational double bogey.

LESSON FOR TODAY

To grow as a golfer (or as a person), it helps if one submits oneself to regular accountability.

Saturday night something odd struck me as I watched members of the left gather on my driving range. Amongst the sixty registered Democrats spread out across the hitting mats, it was the candidates themselves who looked hesitant and confused. From my perch at the window of the pro shop, I watched them and tried to decipher what they were thinking.

I'm antiwar and yet I hold in my hands what is essentially a war club, used to fire these white, nonbiodegradable bullets at a fellow human.

I'm a big believer in protecting the environment, and yet here I am brandishing this 7-iron, taking big divots out of the precious earth, while all around me are gathered people who drive gas-guzzling SUVs, contributing to the global warming that makes all my shots slice to the right. I wonder if I can get away with blaming my slice on global warming?

I continued to observe them and wondered about the purpose of it all, this hiring out of my range for faux political vindication. The only thing I could understand on this night was that my business boomed because the people were given an outlet for election-year stress.

Cack provoked them with the same ease and lack of grace with which he provoked the conservatives. He even drove his cart in reverse. Bullhorn raised, he shouted, "If any of you Dem's actually *win,* your policies will set America back *forty years.* So in your honor I'll drive my cart in like manner."

Thwack. Duff. Whiff. Duff, duff, duff. Thud. Whiff. Thwack . . . Clang.

"Oh for cryin' out loud," Cack hollered. "Who got lucky?"

From the fifth mat, the Democratic candidate for Lieutenant Governor raised his hand and grinned.

Still in reverse, Cack backed in a circle and said, "Give that man a free bucket of balls, Chris. And a free drink too! He loves entitlements so much that we should let him taste one for himself. And while we're at it, let's give free golf balls to all his tree-huggin' friends, plus all the people he bribed on the way to his candidacy."

A frenzy of hurried swings gave me pause to compare the relative abilities of the two camps. The results proved ironic: Republicans tended to swing with more self-righteousness and hit the ball left, while the Democrats swung with privileged annoyance and sliced the ball right.

This irony seemed lost on everyone but Cack, who did not delay in ramming home the point to the throng of GOP bashers. "Aim *right!* Aim *right! If ya wanna whack a conservative, you gotta aim right!*"

Range balls flew in many directions, and once again, aides and volunteers hustled into the pro shop to buy more balls.

My register rang until it hummed. While making change I glanced through the window to watch my groundskeeper going it alone—Molly had left a phone message that she had "other plans." But this was a profitable autumn night, one that would act as ballast for the lean days of winter, and in the fury of fast revenue there was little time to think of romance.

On the TV mounted behind me the debate raged on, the campaigns in full attack mode. From what I'd gathered on the nightly news shows, our nation's highest form of dialogue was no dialogue at all—just one witty sound bite versus another witty sound bite, blurted and repeated and crammed down each other's throats, all for the purpose of acquiring power.

But if America was so polarized that no one ever gave an inch and acted as if destroying your opponent was the only goal worth pursuing, then perhaps Cack had found some middle ground. Perhaps his Taunt-mobile, together with my thirty-six hitting mats and manicured Bermuda, was the stage on which Charlestonians could vent their frustrations in physical form—without actually harming anyone. And perhaps after this reciprocal event, when both sides had swung themselves into exhaustion and were complaining of sore backs, an authentic dialogue would break through the stalemate and allow humans to act, well, human.

Then again, perhaps not.

Near closing time Cack performed what would become his signature move. He stopped in the middle of the range, climbed atop the metal cage, and put his Uncle Sam hat on his head. He faced the left-leaning hackers and raised the bullhorn to his mouth. With his left hand he waved his red, white, and blue hat at the crowd. "Howdy, y'all! I'm a big-spending Republican about to approve funding for oil exploration in the habitat of the spotted owl."

Gasps, tumult, uproar. Violent swings. Cack ducking back into his cart. Buckets upon buckets of golf balls bought with cash, credit card, and righteous indignation.

Once again, Miss Molly's idea had fostered a great night. I figured I owed her a nice dinner, especially since she'd endured my THUMPE test.

Since mid-April I'd been meeting twice per month with two other men to discuss various issues of manhood. We called ourselves Golfers of the Roundtable—our threesome had met each other during a rainout at a local course, and a camaraderie formed as we sat at a round table in the snack bar and shared our backgrounds.

Tonight we met in the downstairs den at the suburban home of Paul Mills, otherwise known as Pauly Three Seeds. His nickname was neither Native American nor Mafia connected. Every bit as Caucasian as myself, Paul was a mild-mannered accountant, complete with white button-down and the occasional pair of navy suspenders. He even drove a minivan. Paul had boasted at our May meeting that he'd had a "male operation," this after fathering three children within the first four years of his marriage. Thus he was dubbed Pauly Three Seeds by the third member of our group, a 280-pound half-Samoan named Benny Tuimatofa.

Benny insisted that nicknames were only appropriate if we each had one, and so he became, at least to himself, Heavy T. They called me Hack, no great surprise there.

"Hack," Benny said as he twisted the cap from a Diet Coke, "today I figured up if people use my nickname ten times per day instead of my full name, over the course of a lifetime I'll save humanity nearly a million syllables."

Benny was big into conservation, except when it came to food.

In the adjoining kitchen I poured a soft drink, and Pauly plopped ice cubes into my glass and urged us to get started.

"I only got an hour," he said, "then I have to go upstairs and help put the kids to bed."

Paul ceded Benny the sofa—which was the only piece of furniture we were confident would hold him. I sat in the recliner, while Pauly opened for himself a folding chair and completed our triangle.

At each meeting we rotated responsibility for introducing a new topic, and tonight was my turn. It struck me as a strange thought at the time, what with my losing the match to Lin and being too embarrassed to tell the guys about it, but I wanted to ask some church-going males what their perspective was on men becoming Passive Adams—if it had anything to do with men and women failing to communicate—so I figured these guys my best bet.

During our summer meetings we'd covered more routine stuff like managing our finances, and now I was about to steer us toward relational topics, which I figured would orbit equally around our threesome, regardless if I were the lone unmarried member.

"Recently I got talked into attending this supposed *relational* course," I explained and grabbed a handful of almonds off the coffee table. "Turns out that a man-hater is using Adam's lack of action in the garden with Eve to promote an all-woman agenda."

Benny nodded and stuffed a pillow behind his back. "My wife says I show a lack of action when it comes to house work."

Without pausing to smile I asked, "So why would a man-hater use that Adam material to slam men?"

Pauly Three Seeds, ever the deep thinker, rubbed his chin and said, "She probably stole it for political purposes. Lots of folks distort things at election time."

Benny raised a finger to make a point. "My wife also accuses me of distorting things."

With faux sympathy I nodded at Benny. "Okay, guys, my question is, can it be true what the man-hater said about Adam affecting all men, that we lack initiative when it comes to relationships?"

Benny's expression turned serious, and he leaned forward on the sofa and lowered his voice, as if what he was about to say was secretive. "Hack, last week my wife tried to get me to attend a class, said it would help me understand the opposite sex. She also threatened not to cook for me next week unless I went. So check this out—I go downtown to sign up for the class, get there ten minutes early, and it's all women, and I mean ALLLL women."

"So you left?" asked Pauly.

"Of course I left," Benny replied. "If there ain't no other dudes in the class, I ain't stayin'."

I squirmed in Pauly's recliner. "That class wasn't held at the Hyatt, was it?"

Benny nodded, sipped his drink. "Yep. And from all I could tell in the two minutes I was there, the lady who was hosting didn't care much for men."

Both of these friends then stared at me as if I were alien.

Pauly said, "Hack, you just turned pale. What's up?"

"Yeah," Benny blurted. "You all right, man? Ate bad almonds?"

I blinked slowly and with embarrassment. "No."

"Then why do you look so out of sorts?"

I wanted to hide under the sofa, though Benny had compressed it to where its crawl space was less than half an inch. "I went to that same class. I was fifteen minutes *late*."

While Pauly got up to refill his drink, Benny eyed me with

a mixture of amusement and concern. "So you left too . . . didn't ya?"

"'Fraid not."

Benny nearly came off the sofa—which was no easy task. "You stayed?! Man, how could you stay?"

"She ticked me off."

"But there weren't any other dudes there, Hack. It was fifty to one."

"Sixty-four to one by the time I introduced myself."

He looked disappointed in me. "What'd they talk about?"

"Mostly about how great Eve was. And still *is.*"

He frowned, shifted his weight on the sofa. "So then you left, right? Bolted out the Hyatt's door?"

This was not the direction I'd intended for tonight's discussion, but I knew there was no way these guys would let the subject pass. I set my glass on the floor and shook my head. "Nope, I stayed till the end. I even got so ticked at her that I made a bet."

Benny covered his eyes with his left hand, as if he knew what was coming next. "Golf bet?" he asked.

"Mmmhmm. And I lost."

Just when I thought Benny would chide me further, he craned his neck and shouted into the kitchen. "Hey, Pauly, get a load o' this: Hack lost a golf match to a woman!"

Pauly re-entered his den and sat again. He crossed his legs to make a space in his lap for his paper plate, and in his calm, measured tone said, "You bet a *woman* at golf? You never told us that."

"This was the one and only time."

"What was the bet?"

My sigh was one part reflection and two parts shame. "I was going to get half the teaching time in her class."

"But you lost."

"I know that. So now I have to attend the rest of the sessions."

Benny and his ample girth resembled an amused vat of Jell-O as he doubled over and laughed. Finally he sat back and said, "Can I come videotape you in class?! Please?"

Pauly waited almost the appropriate amount of time before turning serious again. He resumed his studious composure, and now with hand to chin, index finger tapping his upper lip, he posed a question. "Hack, I don't mean to interrupt your quest to learn all about femininity, but if a single guy like you is asking questions about Adam's lack of initiative, it must be for a specific reason."

I glanced at Benny, met his interested gaze, and nodded. "Her name is Molly."

His expression broadcasted "Ah," but his mouth said, "You've been out with her?"

"Yep."

"And how did that go?" Pauly inquired.

"Pretty well, I think." I blurted my reply, glad to be discussing Molly rather than Lin. "Kinda hard to tell, since the evening ended on an awkward note."

Paul kept tapping that upper lip with his finger, as if he were preparing more questions. I was hoping to avoid more questions. "Mind if I ask you something else?"

Not wanting to offend a buddy, I lied. "Nah...go ahead."

"Did you tell her at the end of the date that you wished to see her again soon?"

"No, I asked her if she wanted to have kids and if she could envision little plastic golf clubs in a crib."

Wide-eyed, Benny appeared stunned at my answer. "Whoa,

man! Little plastic golf clubs in the crib is *not* a first date topic. Little plastic footballs might be okay for a *sixth* date topic, but now you probably scared her off."

Pauly Three Seeds nodded in agreement. "Next time you call her, you'll be lucky if she even answers the phone."

I considered this for all of three seconds. "C'mon, Pauly, now you think you're some sort of dating counselor?"

Pauly smiled with a kind of mild embarrassment. "Hmmm."

Now I was worried that interrogation would never cease. "What do you mean by 'hmmm'?"

"I'm just wondering if instead of 'do you want to have kids and little plastic golf clubs in the crib,' you should've instead told her that you found her interesting and attractive and would enjoy an opportunity to go on a second date."

Though I did not like the relational pressure from Pauly Three Seeds, I felt that I should hear him out. "So, you're saying that I should have been more subtle?"

Benny interrupted Paul. "We're saying that unless you pace things well, a woman might get scared off. When I pursued my wife, I was smooooth."

Paul was eight years older than Benny and me, and in the way of more seasoned citizens he took his time. He even sipped his water with maturity. "Think of it this way, Chris. It's so easy for you to initiate something as quick and unemotional as a golf swing—where the only thing vulnerable is the *ball*. But in contrast, it seems much harder for you to take your time to get to know a woman, where the thing most vulnerable is *two people's futures*."

All three of us stared at the hardwood floor and nodded slowly, in the way men do when they've dived too deep into a subject and can no longer bring themselves to make eye contact.

From my perch in the recliner I tried to steer our chat. "Um, what does all this have to do with Adam?"

Benny said, "In my opinion, Adam ignored his Eve because he was thinking about his golf swing...or something similar."

For a moment we remained silent, male minds trying their best to combine the art of hitting golf balls with the complexities of relationships.

"Hmmm," Paul muttered, still staring at the floor and tapping his lower lip. "That's another deep thought. And a complex one too. Especially when we consider that golf was invented in Scotland in a much later century."

"Yes," Benny said, mocking Paul's super-serious posture. "My opinion about Adam's golf swing is like...water meeting vinegar."

"No," I interjected, "it's like water meeting vinegar mixed with riddles wrapped in enigmas."

"In outer space," said Benny.

"On Friday the thirteenth," added Pauly.

A squealing child from the second floor alerted him that we would likely have to end our meeting early tonight. So we did. Besides, we'd lost control of our main topic, gotten distracted, and now Benny had invaded Pauly's fridge.

I thanked the guys for their advice, told them to stop by the range sometime soon, and was first to leave. On the way home I stopped by my golf shop to check on the night's revenue and to make sure everything was locked up properly.

Cack, as usual, had been very thorough with the closing procedures. The only odd thing I spotted was a note stuck on the door—and it wasn't Cack's handwriting.

Your range should not promote liberalism. Keep that up and my
friends and I will boycott. Or worse.
        —Worried about you.

I wadded the note into a ball and tossed it into a trash
basket, assuring myself that this was from some nongolfing
extremist who knew nothing of what really went on at Hack's.
Have a sense of humor, people.

8

LESSON FOR TODAY

If a match (or a date) is scheduled to start at a specified time, such as 2:00 p.m., the players must be on the first tee (or the doorstep) promptly. Penalty for failing to show is disqualification.

My third visit to the Hyatt began much like the previous two. I ran in late through revolving doors, sweating into my golf shirt and hurrying across the lobby toward Conference Room #4. All day long, a mixture of anxiety and delight had grown within me as I imagined Lin Givens' reaction to my Super Blaster story.

But on this Tuesday night, a young bellhop no more than high school age stood beside the open door. He stared straight ahead, and beyond him I saw the empty conference room. Not even the padded chairs in attendance.

"Did they move the class to another room?" I asked the youngster.

His stoic gaze remained fixed on the far wall. "No."

"Just 'no'? What happened to the class? It was supposed to meet for eight weeks."

"Cops took her."

I stuck my head into the room and reconfirmed its emptiness. "They arrested Lin Givens? What'd she do?"

The kid was a statue. "Can't say. Manager said I can't say."

"C'mon, what'd she do? Just whisper it to me." I moved closer, tilted my head toward him.

"Can't say."

I sighed and turned to leave, wondering what was the best way to dupe a high schooler. "Well, anyway, it'll probably come out in the papers tomorrow or the next day."

I was four steps departed when the bellhop cleared his throat. "Hey."

My turn was slow and calculated. "Yesss?"

"We think she stole campaign money."

"From which party?"

"Can't say."

I raised my eyebrows to get him to say more. I turned my palms outward to request he say more. But he only shook his head.

"C'mon, kid. Please? I lost a golf match to her."

He looked left and right down the hallway. Then he reached inside his bellhop uniform and drew out a folded piece of paper. "Found this note in the room when I was moving the chairs."

I stepped close. "You'll let me read it?"

"If you'll leave me alone."

To all staff,

To accomplish the goals we discussed Sunday night we must make women in the South understand the failure of men as leaders. We must convince women that following male leadership is not the way to progress. We can rise up from within the system, and we can do it by manipulating them just like the serpent manipulated Eve.

We can do it!

LG

In half-hearted acknowledgment I looked up from the note to thank the bellhop, but the kid was already striding for the check-in counter and offering to carry luggage for an elderly couple.

Normally not one to take pleasure in another's problems, I nevertheless smiled as I pictured Lin in a jail cell, with nothing to keep her company but the stories her class had penned the previous week.

With an unexpected free night thrust upon me, I pushed through the revolving door and stepped outside onto the sidewalk. There I plucked my cell phone from my pocket.

Molly answered on the third ring. "Hello?"

"It's me—Chris. Are you still in town?"

She seemed surprised that I had called. "One more day, then off to 'Bama. Are you working late tonight?"

"No, right now I'm at the Hyatt."

"But that's where *I* am. It's where I've been staying all week."

"Well, I'm standing out on the Hyatt's sidewalk."

Short pause. "Am I being stalked by a golf instructor?"

"No."

"Then why are you on the sidewalk of my hotel?"

"The class I told you about, the one taught by the feminist who slanders Adam and wants women to distrust male leaders, it was held here at the Hyatt." I stepped off the sidewalk to let two pedestrians pass. "But class got cancelled."

"Why?"

"Because I think the teacher got arrested."

"For what?"

"Can't say."

"You can trust me, Chris…I'm in politics."

"Yeah…right." I admired the turf on which I stood and wondered why the Hyatt had nicer grass than my driving range. "Wanna grab something to eat?"

The night was no longer young, but middle-aged. On a bench in downtown Charleston, not far from The Battery and the harbor, the two of us ate our ice cream cones and watched the lights dance on the water. Molly had confessed at dinner a not-so-uncommon quirk: Any spicy or salty meal consumed in warm weather must be immediately followed by a search for good ice cream.

"It's like a Democrat rebutting a Republican," she explained between bites. "The sweetness of the dessert rebuts the spices in the dinner."

I ate the last inch of cone and wiped my mouth with a napkin, remembering the Roundtable advice from Pauly and Benny to avoid all mentions of cribs and parenthood on the second date. So, I kept things light. "Do you relate everything to politics?"

Molly took her time, licked her cone. "Only as much as you relate everything to golf."

A small "touché" would hardly suffice. Not with this caliber of woman. "Ya know, Molly, golf is not subjective like politics. In golf, you play a hole and score a four or perhaps a five, but there are never any panels of pundits arguing that the four was really a four and a half, or the five a 5.33, all because so-and-so led a filibuster in the Senate."

She licked a chocolate circle around the apex of her cone. "True, Christopher. But that golf score only matters to the one who hits the ball. Politicians make decisions that matter to the entire populace."

She was not only quick, but logical, and my cone was not only dripping, but onto my shoe. "Maybe so, but golf reveals a person's character, their patience under stress. Politics hides character because the first priority is to gain votes."

She gazed across the harbor for all of two seconds. "Point taken, but remember this: the stars on the American flag represent fifty states governed by laws created by politicians; the stars do not represent fifty holes-in-one made by a bunch of no-name hackers."

I am losing. I am definitely not Superman. The way she made her points, not to mention the speed with which she conjured them, reminded me of why I never excelled at debate. But in an attempt to stay competitive I pursed my lips, crossed my legs, and said, "Politicians lie."

She never flinched. "Golfers cheat."

"Politicians can't putt."

"Golfers can't amend the Constitution."

"Politicians talk in circles."

"Golfers dress funny."

Just to amuse her I feigned a self-conscious glance at my clothes. "You don't like the way I dress? I thought earth tones were all the rage."

For the first time since we'd met, Molly appeared taken aback, at a loss for what to say. She rubbed the sole of her shoe on the grass, and after an awkward silence, even her voice sounded reserved. "The way you dress is fine, Chris. Really. It's just that I was trying to keep our chat light, especially since last time when you asked me about kids and cribs and stuff."

Her ice cream had begun to drip, and I pulled an extra napkin from my pocket and handed it to her. "I had a similar motivation tonight," I confessed. "To not sound so aggressive."

She wiped her fingers and spoke between licks of her cone. "Then why did you bring up all that parenthood stuff the other night?"

I held my own cone at arm's length and allowed a couple of drops to fall to the ground. "I think I was just trying to mimic a friend of mine who signed up for an Internet dating site two years ago. He put at the top of his profile in big letters, 'IF YOU DO NOT WANT TO HAVE KIDS, PLEASE DO NOT CONTACT ME, AS I AM ALREADY CERTAIN THAT YOU ARE NOT MY SOUL MATE.'"

Molly smiled and shook her head, as if this method was just a wee bit much. "Well, did it work?"

"He married the first woman he went out with. They just had twin girls."

She mouthed a silent "wow" and returned her gaze to the harbor. After a few more licks of her cone she added, "I'm glad we're not talking about politics anymore, Mister Chris."

"And I'm glad we're not talking about golf anymore, Miss Molly."

She began whittling down the top of her cone with a series of small bites. After she'd chewed and swallowed, she said, "By the way, if you ever blurt out 'Good golly, Miss Molly' in a Little Richard-like voice, I will probably never speak to you again."

I'm so glad she told me that. I was waiting for just the right moment. . . .

"So you've heard that line many times?"

She wiped her fingers and frowned in the moonlight.

"From many, many men who thought they were very, very original."

"Didn't work for you?"

She wriggled her left ring finger. "Still single, aren't I?" She adjusted her posture and scooted an inch closer to me. "By the way, have you whacked any conservatives this week?"

"Thanks to you, yes. They keep coming back, as do the Democrats."

We finished our cones and told each other again how good it all was. But it felt strange to allow this rendezvous to pass without ever talking of anything more substantial, especially with her leaving town soon.

After another long moment of silence, she shifted her posture on the bench and turned slightly away from me to stare across the harbor. "The moon is pretty tonight."

This celestial detour to our chat caught me by surprise. To agree with her moon comment felt obvious, and somewhat dumb. To disagree felt very dumb. And so I said nothing. And so she said nothing.

We just sat there gazing at the moon and its rippling reflection. I wondered if she wanted to talk on a deeper level, if she was waiting for me to begin. But I was not going to pressure her and mention again my desire to have children, so all I did was keep looking out at the harbor and the moonlight. The one boat that eased by in the distance seemed a kind of buoyant relief, something to cause us to turn in sync and follow it for long minutes.

Finally Molly tilted her head toward me. "So, Golf Man really wants to be a father, eh?"

I paused—not to think about my answer but simply not to appear too eager. "Yep, someday." I let my reply linger in the night air before returning the question. "So, does Miss Political Analyst really want to be a mom?"

She too waited a moment to answer. "Someday, yes."

Sometime later I walked Molly to her rental car. She surprised me when she hugged me good-bye. "I leave for Alabama tomorrow, Chris. But if you'd like to call me some evening, you have my cell number."

To summon perfect words of departure seemed a skill I did not possess. So I simply returned her hug. "How about if I call you in three days?"

"Sounds great." After she'd unlocked the door, she turned and said, "Thanks for the Thai food and ice cream."

"And thank you for the increase in golf ball sales due to political venting." I reached for her door and swung it wide.

She smiled and got into the car but left the door open. "If you ever need any more ideas on how to exploit divisiveness, just call me. It's an outflow of my crazy job."

This was unexpected, this double invitation to contact her. "I'll do that."

She stuck her key in the ignition and smiled up at me, both of us still chatty in the way people are when they aren't sure how to say good-bye. "Well, I gotta go prepare for tomorrow. I'm moving up from state elections to Senate and House campaigns. In 'Bama I might even get to shake hands with the president."

I couldn't think of anything better to say, so I just said the first thing that came to mind. "Well, tell him he can visit my range if he's in the area. I give free lessons to all presidents, regardless of skill."

Molly closed her door and lowered her window. "You're a good guy, Chris Hackett."

The red of her taillights sufficed as a last wave good-bye.

I walked back around the sidewalk of the Battery, paralleling the harbor on the way to my truck. But I didn't want to leave just yet, so above the docile waters I leaned against the barrier railing and replayed the end to tonight's date.

"You're a good guy, Chris Hackett"?

What does that *mean* in girl-speak?

9

LESSON FOR TODAY

Never underestimate the tendency of other
players to copy a new fad. Such fads may
arise in the realm of new equipment, new
lingo, style of dress, even a new method of
snubbing rivals.

In a land obsessed with equality, it was bound to happen. Some
other group was bound to hear of the two political parties having a go at each other on my golf range, and of course this new
group would request equal time.

At six p.m. on Thursday, eleven members of the Charleston
Atheist Party walked into my pro shop, golf bags over shoulders, faithless grins on their faces. I knew they were members
of said party because they all wore gray shirts with *Charleston
Atheist Party* embroidered on the pocket. For people who turned
up their noses at organized religion, they seemed quite organized around their own.

After pleasant but brief introductions, one of them, a tall,
slender man in his forties, took over as spokesman. "We'd
like to express ourselves on your driving range," he said,
blank-faced.

I managed a half-smile across my counter. "Express yourselves?"

"Yes. Like the Democrats and Republicans got to do last week. We have cash for twenty-two buckets of balls. Two for each of us." He plucked from his pocket a roll of twenties.

"Who do you want to hit golf balls at...liberals or conservatives?"

He turned to his fellow party members and exchanged knowing smiles.

"Actually neither," he said, leaning into the counter now. "We were kind of hoping that you could find a loudmouth religious person—perhaps a Pentecostal or a Southern Baptist or even a Mormon—to drive the golf cart around and taunt us."

I raised a finger of reservation. *Just a moment, sir.* From beneath the counter I grabbed my walkie-talkie and called Cack down in the maintenance shed. "Cack...you there?"

Silence.

I tried again. "Yo, Cackster!...Your services are needed."

"What now?" he asked. "The TV went out again?"

"No, I need you to grab your bullhorn and shout fire an' brimstone to eleven atheists."

Very short pause. "You what?"

"They just bought twenty-two buckets of balls...so dinner is on me if you can pull this off."

Very long pause. "Are they charismatic atheists or just normal atheists?"

"Let me ask."

I asked.

"Cack?" I said into the walkie-talkie.

"Yeah?"

"They're normal atheists."

His chuckle preceded my embarrassment. Cack said, "I was only kidding, Chris. Gimme five minutes to ready the cart."

I suppose this was to be expected, this business of equal time. Who knew what other polarized groups would show up. Animal Rights versus NRA? Red Sox fans versus Yankees? Union versus Confederacy?

My theory proved true, though my examples weren't local enough. Just minutes after the atheists manned the hitting mats, the blond high school girl who'd requested my services on the night of Whack the Liberal sashayed into the pro shop. And I do mean *sashayed*.

"Remember me?" she asked, batting eyelashes too young for such battage.

"Um, yes," I stammered, "you're the conservative teenager who refuses to dress conservatively."

Giggles. More battage. "Yes, well, I was just wondering . . ."

Please don't ask me for private golf lessons . . . please oh please no.

"Yes?" I inquired.

She moved closer, pink fingernails stroking the countertop. "I was wondering, since next weekend is the football rivalry between Burke and Hanahan, if some of my high school friends and I could, like, rent out your driving range . . . and maybe, like, dress up the cart as our rival?"

Visions of teenage chaos competed with visions of increased revenue. "Which team is your rival?"

"Burke, silly! I'm a Hanahan girl all the way!" She blurted this with all the overenthusiasm of a sixteen-year-old.

"Of course you are," I said. "Can you hold on one sec?"

"Okay." She tapped her fingernails on my counter while I called Cack on the two-way. "Cack?"

Five seconds later he answered. "Yeah, boss?"

"Can you also be a local mascot—perhaps the Burke Bulldog?"

"Now you want me to impersonate a *dog*? Whaddaya want me to do, drive around the range with a pooper-scooper and bark?"

After I ended the call to Cack with a "ten-four," the blond teenager told me she could fill the mats to full capacity, that she and her pep rally friends would number between eighty and one hundred—not including alumni.

"How much would two hundred buckets of range balls cost?" she asked, adding two more bouts of batting lashes, which I took as her request for a discount.

I reminded myself that I was thirty-one and calmly reached for my calculator. "Seven dollars per bucket…times two hundred…is fourteen hundred dollars," I said, stunned that I was quoting such figures to a high schooler. Perhaps she had rich parents. "But I can give you a discount. How about five-fifty per bucket?"

She pulled out a credit card. "Oh, thank you soooo much! My dad said to rent out the entire range if you would let us and for me to pay in advance. All my friends will pay me back next week."

She swiped her father's Visa in my card machine, and just like that, Hack's Golf Learning Center gained eleven hundred dollars in sales.

Word had spread among the Charleston golfing community— and even outside the golfing community—that Hack's was the most entertaining golf range in the city and that it was a great place to vent frustrations at our polarized world. This momentum was largely fueled by Cack, who promoted our business at every restaurant he frequented, sharing with total strangers his opinions on the world and its many corners of bias.

Together we had no problem exploiting those biases for the sake of revenue. This was America, where bias, like most everything else, was a commodity to be bought or sold—or milked for personal advantage.

My growing fear, however, was that soon I'd have no more normal students—only liberals who despised conservatives, conservatives who despised liberals, atheists who despised Christians, and Christians who wouldn't fire back because they were convinced that Jesus would never hit golf balls at pagans. This point was rammed home to me by both Benny and Pauly Three Seeds, who a week earlier had tried to get their Sunday school class to sign up for "Whack the Heathen" night, but got only one signee and thus cancelled the event.

Out on the range, Cack weaved in front of the atheists and raised the bullhorn to his lips. "Okay, you godless bunch of hackers, this cart is my rolling bully pulpit, and I'm about to start preachin'. . . ."

And all the people did not say "Amen."

Saturday morning at Hack's I hosted a "Couple's Special" for beginners. For the past week I'd advertised an opportunity for husband and wife to learn the game together, and this for only twenty-five bucks per couple.

Out on the hitting mats, seven couples—young and old, coordinated and uncoordinated—swatted away as I moved behind each and instructed them on stance, grip, and alignment. A morning fog had lifted from the Charleston coastline, and now the sun shone bright and warm, an ideal day to be outdoors.

Minutes into the lesson a pattern emerged: The women accepted instruction eagerly, though most of the men thought they could figure things out for themselves. Fortunately, corrective comments from the wives helped bring the men back to reality. From the line of mats came everything from, "Listen to Mr. Hackett, dear, he's a professional," to the more blunt and shrill, "Pay attention, Herb! You don't know what you're doing!"

I was doing my best to use marital metaphors—"Marry your arm swing to your hip rotation" seemed to work wonders for all—when an eighth couple, this one thirtyish and energetic, rushed through my pro shop and out to the range to join us.

"Sorry we're a few minutes late," the man said. He introduced himself as Steve. His wife—a tall blond who introduced herself as Darcy—shook my hand and asked if I had any rental clubs.

"Included with the lessons," I said and pointed to a bag full of clubs I'd set out behind the group.

They selected their weapons, and I pointed them to the ninth and tenth hitting mats, where Steve shook his head at the fake turf and announced that he wanted to learn on *real grass*. "I've never seen a pro hit off mats," he boasted to his wife.

She rolled her eyes as if she'd heard it all before. "Just do as the instructor advises, honey."

He stood on the tenth mat and stretched his back. She did the same on the ninth.

To this day those two remain the worst golfers I have ever seen. Anywhere. At any time. Throughout my history of owning a golf range and giving lessons, they are hands down the most uncoordinated pair to ever dent the Bermuda. After the rest of the group had completed their lessons and departed, I worked with each of them for an extra fifteen minutes. I covered and recovered the basics of proper stance, grip, and backswing—and yet Steve still missed the ball completely. For eight straight swings he whiffed.

Darcy outwhiffed him by a nearly two-to-one ratio. She missed the ball fifteen times before finally making unsolid contact, a low dribbler that nearly hit her hubbie in the ankle.

"This is not as much fun as I thought," she said after six more misses.

After ten more she said they'd had enough. He paid me twenty-five bucks, and they walked in front of me to the pro shop and toward the exit and the pea gravel. At the door she said something about how she'd rather try surfing, that they had a friend who'd give them free lessons.

"Surfing is so much more subjective than golf," she said to her husband. "Plus I won't sweat as much."

He nodded his agreement and pushed open my glass door. "Anything you say, honey."

Part of my job was to accept that some people are naturally coordinated for the sport of golf, and some not. Some people try it once and give it up out of frustration. Some try it twice before doing the same.

I took no offense from Darcy and Steve. Rather, as I watched them stroll across the parking lot hand-in-hand, I grew envious of their relationship; they were simply two uncoordinated people in love. I wondered if Molly and I would ever get to their level. What I wasn't envious of was their car. Some kind of old Cadillac, painted a hideous shade of green. To each his own. South Carolina had long been known for its eccentric citizens.

At closing time, Cack and I gathered again at the pro shop counter, going through our end-of-day routine and counting the money. In midcount he paused to turn on our TV. Amused at the emotional banter blaring overhead, we occasionally glanced up to watch the politicians have a go at each other. The elections were only six weeks away, and the debates had become heated.

What I did not expect was to see my favorite sport exploited on the local campaign trail. It had even become fashionable to use golf lingo.

One guy running for state senator worked a crowd on the campus of the College of Charleston. As TV cameras moved in for close-up shots, he even made a slow motion golf swing. Then he shouted into the mic, "My opponent consistently triple bogeys the issue of school vouchers, and his stance on immigration is a water hazard in itself. My opponent will gamble with your tax dollars, so swing for the green with Senator Schilling."

Cack stared up at the TV and muttered the obvious. "Man, that is so cheesy."

10

LESSON FOR TODAY

While competing in the game, the only person who can offer advice to the player is his or her caddie. Off the course, however, advice may be sought from anyone—and if this person happens to be an expert in a crucial area of the game, the wise player listens with great attentiveness.

Pauly Three Seeds was as exacting with his golf clubs as he was with his accounting profession. Today on his lunch hour he came into the shop to pay for the putter he'd asked me to alter. I supposed that some men just obsess over their possessions, and Pauly was no exception. In July he'd paid me to regrip his irons—"They're too thin," he'd insisted—and then in August he'd had me change the shafts in his woods. "They're too flexible." The putter issue was even more precise: "Add two degrees of loft," he'd requested. "It'll make my putts roll smoother."

"When do you even have time to *play*?" I asked and set his club on the counter. "You have three little kids to raise."

"That's just it, Hack. I hardly ever play anymore. But when I do, I want my clubs to fit, like a good tux."

Pauly handed me a MasterCard, and I swiped it and handed him a receipt to sign. A tall man, he stooped and leaned over my counter to pen his name. "Whatever happened with that Molly woman you told us about the other night?" he asked in midsignature.

"She left town yesterday."

He plucked his copy of the receipt from the counter and tucked it into his shirt pocket. The way he stood there, looking down at me and nodding, told me that he had picked today to try to gather a few more facts about my personal life. "Mind if I ask you something?"

I handed him his club and frowned. "We're in an accountability group together, Pauly. You're free to ask anything."

He stood erect and stepped back from the counter. "Yes, I suppose I am. So, did you make it clear to her before she left town that you find her attractive and would enjoy an opportunity to get to know her further?"

This was a bit more than I expected, and suddenly my hope was that more customers would tromp through the pea gravel, enter the shop, and interrupt us. But early afternoon on Thursdays was usually a slow time, and my range remained empty. "Yep, I did. I also avoided pressuring her about the kids issue, if that's what you were going to ask next. I've been thinking about how I could go visit her on the campaign trail, but I can't just up and leave my range, especially during the fall season when business is great."

Hand on chin, Pauly assumed the posture of the deep thinking. Then he plucked a pair of golf balls from a plastic bucket I'd set out on the counter. For a moment he rolled the golf balls around in his palms, staring at them as if debating their significance in the grand scheme of things. "If I were you, Hack, I'd try to see her sooner than later. I mean, you'd be shocked at how far her mind has run ahead of yours. I'd wager that she's already trying out your last name."

Refusing to believe him, I shook my head and fiddled with the coins in my cash register. "No way."

"Yes way. What's her full name?"

"Molly Elizabeth Cusack."

He put a finger to his lips, narrowed his eyes. Finally he set the two golf balls back into the plastic bucket. "I'd bet that she's already stood in front of a mirror and whispered 'Molly Elizabeth Hackett' at least five times."

Now it was my turn to play with the golf balls. "You're scarin' me, Pauly."

He turned and looked out the glassed entrance. In the now busy parking lot, parents were dropping off kids and unloading golf bags from SUVs. "You have lessons to give?" he asked.

I nodded. "Junior high guys at four. Junior high girls at four forty-five."

"Then we'll discuss this at our next meeting. Meanwhile, Hack, look in the mirror tonight and repeat to yourself, 'Molly Elizabeth Hackett, Molly Elizabeth Hackett!' "

His wide grin was out of nature for him, as was the sudden sense of humor. And yet, as Pauly Three Seeds strolled out my door with his newfangled putter, I didn't know whether to feel encouraged or worried. Too many thoughts collided, and they came in pairs. Molly thoughts and golf thoughts, fatherhood thoughts and manhood thoughts. One more accompanied me out to the range, where five junior high boys were trying to hit golf balls while hopping on one leg.

Why doesn't my range attract any normal people?

11

LESSON FOR TODAY

The game is played at many socioeconomic levels.
Though amenities at the country club level may
be far superior, polling data suggests that more
spontaneous fun happens at the public level.

I did not expect the country music crowd. Early on Friday
night, the Bubbas and the Mary Lous, their twangy songs and
their pickup trucks, all gathered in my parking lot. The scene
was yet another first for Hack's: tobacco pouches stuffed into
pockets; Hank Williams T-shirts tucked into jeans held up
with enormous belt buckles; and golf shoes nastier than Merle
Haggard's spittoon.

More than twenty of them crowded into my pro shop
and pressed against the counter. "Big ones," said the largest
Bubba. He pulled a wadded bill from his pocket and handed
it to me.

I accepted his crumpled twenty and tucked it into the register. "You want to purchase large buckets of golf balls?"

"Big ones." He then turned to his mass of silver-buckled
groupies and said, "Ever'body wants big ones, right?"

Ever'body said, "Yep, 'at's right."

He motioned to them with his massive right arm. "Then gets yer cash up here and give it to this city slicker."

They gots their cash up to me, and I gots each of them a large bucket of balls.

As they passed through my shop and out to the hitting mats, I noticed that nearly half of them had not bothered with wearing golf shoes at all; in fact, they had no reservations about practicing golf in cowboy boots.

They spread out among the mats, occupying all but eight. After a few minutes of watching them struggle, I walked outside behind the mats and asked if anyone wanted a free five-minute lesson—my attempt to build customer loyalty.

Their replies were all negative, though creative in a rural kind of way.

"Naw, reckon not."

"'Ats a'ight."

One bearded guy pointed his club at me and said, "This dawg already hunts."

And then, way down on the thirty-first mat, the biggest Bubba took a mighty swing and shouted "Yeeee Hawww!" as a range ball launched into a slicing orbit.

They all seemed to be doing fine without me, so I returned to the shop. Waiting for me inside was a smaller and quite different group. Five youths in baggy jeans, gold chains, and New Balance sneakers.

"What a man gotta do to hit golf balls here?" their leader inquired.

"Large buckets are seven dollars," I said. "Medium is five."

In place of a verbal reply he nodded and turned his cap sideways. His four friends did likewise.

"No golf clubs, guys?" I asked, noticing that none of the five had a golf bag.

Their spokesman glanced around my shop at the merchandise. "Nah, ain't none of us got clubs."

I pointed to the bag of spare clubs I kept in the corner of my shop. "We have some extras we loan out. No problem . . ."

He went over and plucked a child-sized club from the bag but quickly rejected it. "Got any of those big-headed clubs?"

"You mean titanium drivers?"

"Yeah, drivers. We wanna blast some drivers."

I informed them that the Bubbas and the Mary Lous had borrowed all but one of my spare titanium drivers. Yet the youth still purchased three large buckets of balls. Before they could get through the shop and push open the door to the range, however, my curiosity surfaced. "By the way, guys, are you college students or what?"

The shortest one tugged the bill of his cap down and said, "Naw man, we're doctors. Doctors of cool."

At the door all heads nodded. "MDs of hip-hop," said the fifth doc.

I dug deep for customer relation skills. "That's fine, guys. Good to have some doctors at my range." I caught the skeptical glance of their leader. "By the way, what is your name...Doctor what?"

He turned and smiled at his friends. "I don't go by no doctor name, man. They call me Tongue Depressuh."

I reached across the counter and shook his hand. "Welcome to Hack's, Mister Depressuh."

He smiled, and the look in his eyes told me his name held meanings that were far beyond my understanding.

Out on the range, they gathered at the tenth mat, firing away in between a host of Bubbas, who swung the titanium drivers with such force that their T-shirts had pulled out from their jeans. The diversity of my range pleased me; this too was good for business.

My hope was that none of these customers would ask me to supply someone to drive around in the cart and insult them. Not that Cack couldn't pull it off, mind you. Probably some lines about the youth's gold jewelry coming from a Cracker Jack box. And then some reciprocal insults for the Bubbas, something to do with cow patties.

This was Cack's day off, however, so all customers had the privilege of practicing without harassment.

Thirty minutes later Mrs. Dupree strolled in to my shop, this time without her one-brick dog. She donned red capri pants, a red golf shirt, and sunglasses much too big for her face. She didn't have her golf clubs with her, so I figured this was a social call.

Mrs. Dupree had a habit of skipping pleasantries and just getting straight to the point. She thrust an international envelope over my cash register and waited for me to rise from my chair and accept it. "Read that, Chris. It touched my heart."

"Who's it from?"

"Ground troops in Iraq. I figured you may want to help."

I propped my elbows on the counter and read the letter.

Dear Mrs. Dupree,

My platoon can't thank you enough for the three hundred golf balls you sent us back in June. Those, plus the clubs you sent, have kept our spirits up. We are still stuck in the desert awaiting orders, some four hundred miles from Baghdad. The days here are long, so for recreation we built a golf course in the desert. We buried coffee cans at 150-yard intervals and stuck tent poles in them and hung red do-rags on the poles for flags.

We use our helmets as tee markers. The reason I am writing is to let you know that I scored my first ever hole-in-one yesterday. My shot hit the top of a dune, hung on the slope for a second, then rolled down the sand and into the coffee can. Fortunately, I did not have to buy beers for the other players because we have no beer.

Unfortunately, half of our platoon has never played golf, so we are already down to just fourteen golf balls from the original three hundred. By the time this letter gets to you, I am sure we will have lost these as well. Anyway, fourteen balls is not enough for a hundred thirty soldiers who somehow cannot learn to share. Could you please send another few hundred balls? And could you send orange ones? (They're easier to find in the dunes.)

Many thanks,
Corporal Bryant,
Ground Maintenance
IRAQ

P.S. Our only casualty so far came two nights ago when Sergeant Harris thought the enemy was sneaking up. He fired three M-16 rounds through Corporal Gomez's helmet. Luckily, Corporal Gomez was sound asleep in our tent, and his bullet-riddled helmet lay out on a sand dune, still in use as the tee marker for our seventh hole.

The letter struck a patriotic chord in me. I had never thought of such needs. I'd just assumed our overseas soldiers spent their entire days either fighting the enemy, planning how to fight the enemy, or eating bad food inside mess tents while talking about fighting the enemy.

I tapped my index finger on the letter and met Mrs. Dupree's hopeful gaze. "The military requests orange golf balls?"

She picked up the letter and motioned to the requested item. "Yes. But I just left Wal-Mart and they're all out of orange ones. So I bought orange magic markers instead. I figure you and I could stripe some golf balls orange. Wouldn't that work?"

"Are they permanent markers?"

"Yes."

"Then yes, you could put thick orange stripes on 'em. I guess you want me to donate a few hundred balls?"

Mrs. Dupree looked shocked. "Oh, not at all!" Then she pointed out the glass doors to her Mercedes. "I bought thirty dozen white ones. The Wal-Mart manager gave me a deal after I told him how our soldiers get bored sitting in that hot desert. Don't you think we could stripe them today?"

"You mean right *now*? I'm not an army supply store, Mrs. Dupree."

Mrs. Dupree moved around my counter to where she could see the range full of customers. She squinted into the afternoon sun and said, "You could ask for volunteers."

"But I don't want to disturb my customers. Look at them, they're all swatting away, all of them happy. They wouldn't want to get involved."

Mrs. Dupree frowned the frown of a woman who did not know the meaning of no. She hitched her red capri pants a bit and came striding around my counter. "Does that intercom system work?"

"Works fine. Why?"

She moved past me, which was difficult in the tight space behind the counter. "Do you mind?"

"We can't just—"

Next to the cash register she grabbed the mic and made her announcement to my customers. At the first squawk of the loudspeakers, country and hip-hop all paused from their swings to listen. "ANYONE WHO IS PATRIOTIC AND WISHES TO EARN A FREE BUCKET OF RANGE BALLS PLEASE PROCEED TO THE MAINTENANCE SHED. WE'LL BE SENDING GOLF BALLS TO GROUND TROOPS IN IRAQ."

To my amazement, three Mary Lous, four Bubbas, and all five of the hip-hop youth set down their clubs and made their way to the shed.

Mrs. Dupree turned to me. "Say it with me, Chris. I was—"

"Wrong?"

"Of course you were." She set the mic back in its stand, and we hurried out to her car to fetch the supplies.

Perhaps patriotism still united Americans. At the open garage door of the maintenance shed, I handed out boxes of white golf balls to each volunteer, while Mrs. Dupree distributed orange permanent markers. Down there on the concrete floor, Bubbas and Mary Lous sat beside Tongue Depressuh and friends, all of them with markers in hand, all of them concentrating on their task.

When we finished I jogged back to my shop and checked e-mail. I had three from equipment sales reps and one from Molly:

I only have a few seconds, Chris, but wanted to say hi! If I had to sum up the day in 'Bama in one sentence, it'd be: "Conservatives and liberals yelling half-truths into microphones." How about your day?

—M

I replied in kind.

My day in one sentence? *"Ebony and ivory, striping golf balls*
in perfect harmony."
      Talk soon,
      —C

12

LESSON FOR TODAY

**The game of golf and the game of life
are expensive for their operators, and
one is just as vulnerable to inflation
as the other.**

I did not own the land on which Hack's subsisted. The real
estate was leased from a local developer, a Mr. Vignatti. I paid
him $1,950 per month to lease my part of his property. Next
door to me sat twenty acres of plants and shrubs and daylilies,
the product in trade of Roycroft Nurseries.

Charleston's propensity for elaborate home gardens kept
Mr. Roycroft in the big time. He, too, leased his land from
Mr. Vignatti. I rarely got to visit with the balding Mr. Roycroft,
except of course when a few stray range balls found their way over
my perimeter netting and into his plants. He always returned the
balls in a plastic bag—sometimes eight or ten balls, sometimes a
few dozen. He'd leave the bags at my doorstep, and in apprecia-
tion I'd call and tell him to come hit a complimentary bucket.

Today Mr. Roycroft and I sat next to each other on the third
floor of an office tower, occupying one side of a rectangular
conference table as we faced our landlord, Mr. Vignatti.

Mr. V looked like an Italian mob boss, though the pink stationery in his briefcase and the yellow-framed family photos adorning his walls did nothing to further that image. The three of us met once per quarter, mostly to "talk about numbers." Mr. Vignatti, of course, did the talking.

He opened a leather binder and drew out his record of lease payments. I knew my payments were punctual; I mailed them to him on the fifteenth of each month.

"Chris," he said, "you have made all payments on time…and this is a good thing."

Then he turned to Mr. Roycroft. "Mr. Roy, you too have made all payments on time, and this also is a good thing."

Mr. Roycroft nodded and smiled but made no attempt to correct Mr. V's calling him "Mr. Roy." I did likewise. The two of us had been through this so many times that we knew not to make conversation unless it was necessary.

Mr. Vignatti pulled what looked like government papers from his leather binder. Already he was frowning at the top sheet. "I have new tax bills, gentlemen. And yes, of course there is increase. Every year…increase! Never decrease. The politicians always vote yes and yes for more property tax, never no." He assumed the stern look of an agitated professor. "I tell you both, this country of ours will one day collapse from all the yes to tax increase."

Again, Mr. Roycroft and I both nodded in agreement.

Mr. Vignatti preened his mustache, eyed us both. "And of course this will mean higher leases for you…which I suppose is a bad thing."

Mr. Roycroft and I sat up straight at his utterance of "bad thing."

Mr. V then directed his attention at me. "Chris, I am not so sure about the political golf ball whacking that you allow on my land. This could cause problems, no?"

I quickly shook my head. "No problems, Mr. Vignatti. You see, I've balanced it to where all sides have equal access."

Expressionless, he rubbed his mustache a second time, then a third. Then he sighed audibly. "This equal access…this is a good thing for your business, yes?"

I had the feeling that in Mr. Vignatti's world, every event was either a good thing or a bad thing, but never a mediocre thing or an average thing or, even on a cloudy day, a gray thing.

Mr. Vignatti produced a calculator. "Chris," he said, his index finger hovering over the buttons, "your average month before the politics was $7,800 in sales, is this correct?"

I felt a bit embarrassed that he was quoting the figures in front of Mr. Roycroft, who humbly stared at the floor, as if he knew this was not the best way to handle things.

"Yessir, that is correct."

"And what will be your monthly estimate while the political types inhabit your business?"

"I'm estimating over nine, sir."

"Over nine thousand…" He turned and winked at Mr. Roycroft. "This Chris is doing okay for himself, yes?"

"Appears so," said Mr. Roycroft. He turned to me with a look of sympathy and shrugged, as if to say, "This is what we have to put up with for leasing from this guy."

I could only shrug back and hope this meeting would end soon. I'd been through this more than twenty times in six years, and the protocol never changed, just the numbers and the number of times Mr. Vignatti ended his statements with an Italian "yes?" or "no?"

Mr. Vignatti then addressed Mr. Roycroft. "And you, Mr. Roy, your average month has been $10,700 for this year…this is correct, no?"

Mr. Roycroft blushed at the recitation of his revenue. I leaned toward him and gave him a gentle elbow in the ribs. "Congrats, you capitalistic stud."

Mr. Vignatti overheard my comment and furrowed his brow. "What is the meaning of this…this 'capitalistic stud' business?" He looked very confused.

Mr. Roycroft had his hand over his mouth, trying not to laugh.

I met Mr. Vignatti's worrisome gaze. "I just meant that Mr. Roycroft is good at selling plants, that he sells more plants than I sell golf balls."

Mr. Vignatti eased back in his chair. A trace of a smile lifted the tips of his mustache. "You congratulate your neighbor.…This is a good thing, Chris. But the truth here is that Mr. Roycroft operates on forty percent more land."

Again the calculator was pushed to the center of the table. He pressed more buttons. "It appears that golf balls are selling slightly better per acre than plants. This gives me confusion."

Oh no, don't give Mr. Vignatti confusion. Anything but that. Good things might become bad things.

Mr. Roycroft winced. "But I pay you on time every month, Mr. Vignatti."

Mr. V closed his leather binder and rested his hands atop it. "This is true. Even when the hurricane destroys your rhodo…what is that plant name?"

"Rhododendron, sir. Everything else was wiped out as well."

"Yes, even when the hurricane destroys all the Roycroft plantings, you pay in full and on time. This was a good thing."

He winked at me, as if I should agree that this was good. So I winked back and added a smile.

Mr. Vignatti then placed both hands over his calculator. "But now I have this issue of the taxes, of which man should pay more?" He paused to point at us, waving his finger back and forth. "Who...Mr. Golf Ball or Mr. Rhododendron? This is the question that haunts me."

"Mr. Vignatti," I inquired with great gentleness of voice, "how much of an increase in property taxes are you facing?"

Mr. Vignatti kept his left hand over the calculator, to where we could not see his number crunching. Finally he lifted his hand and showed us the number: $188.40.

Mr. Roycroft stared at the number, as if amazed at its smallness. "One-eighty-eight more per month? For each of us?"

"No, this increase is per year. And so this is the total of increase." He divided the number by two, and again showed us the total: $94.20. "You each can agree to this increase, I assume?"

Mr. Roycroft and I exchanged a glance of relief.

"I can certainly handle a ninety-four dollar increase in yearly rent," I said.

"And so can I," Mr. Roycroft added quickly.

Mr. Vignatti stood and plucked his leather binder from the table. He tucked it under his left arm and grinned at both of us, his signal that our little business meeting was about to adjourn.

I stood too, as did Mr. Roycroft. Neither of us knew what to say. I figured that he too wanted to get back to his businesses; we were surely losing more than the tiny tax increase by hanging out here with Mr. V.

I cleared my throat and said, "Mr. Vignatti, are there any more issues you wish to talk through today?"

He wagged a finger at me. "You just be careful with the politics, Chris. We do not want any trouble for the Vignatti name."

"Yessir. No trouble at all. Only fairness."

Mr. Roycroft opened the conference room door, and I followed him out. Behind us came the departing words from Mr. V. "Fairness, Chris...this too is a good thing."

Back at Hack's I commenced to filling plastic buckets with golf balls, optimistic that some customers might show up on this very slow day. After I'd filled ten buckets I looked through the back window and spotted out on the grass a lone golfer. She was taking practice swings at the far end of the range, and near her feet lay a jumbo bucket of balls.

At first I didn't recognize her—she was quite a distance away—but soon the pace of her swing, together with her short haircut, triggered familiarity. Lin Givens had invaded my range. Once again she wore black pants, though this time her top was a soft gray, her golf shoes white.

Immediately I grabbed the walkie-talkie and called Cack down in the maintenance shed. "Cackster, did ya see who's out on the range?"

It took him a few seconds to reply. "Yep. She came in just before you got back from your meeting."

"But I thought she went to jail." I pointed at her through the glass. "What's she doing *here*?"

"Beats me, boss. She just said she wanted to hit some golf balls and relieve some stress."

"So you actually sold her some of our golf balls?"

"At half price. She had a coupon."

I had to know more. Out of the pro shop I went, walking purposefully toward Lin, my 5-iron in hand just in case we ended up making another bet.

She saw me coming, paused in midswing, and rested her club on her shoulder. "Are you going to insist that I leave, Chris?"

I stopped some ten feet from her, an awkward distance that somehow felt right, given the circumstances. "Why'd you come here?"

She reached out with her club and rolled a ball into place and struck it accurately toward the 100-yard marker. The ball flew high and upon reentry plugged into moist turf. "I just wanted to hit some golf balls, get rid of some stress."

Her tone was surprisingly reserved, conversational even. I felt tensions ease and stepped a couple feet closer, to where only one hitting mat separated us. "A bellhop at the Hyatt said the cops took you."

She nodded, rolled another ball onto the mat with her club. "Did he tell you that they were women cops? Friends of mine?"

"No."

"Did he tell you that they were not arresting me but protecting me?"

"He said you may have stolen campaign monies."

She shook her head and exchanged her club for a longer one. "Someone made a death threat against me. The campaign money thing was just an excuse to get me out of the Hyatt."

I had no idea what to say. She sounded sincere, and I couldn't blame someone from bolting from a class if her life was threatened. "So your class is really cancelled? For good?"

Lin nodded, grabbed a towel from her golf bag. She wiped dirt from her club and admired its sheen. "If you must know, Chris, I was being paid by a radical faction to try to woo female voters. But it wasn't going well. And you should also know that I'm not quite as radical as I came off in class."

She swung harder this time, and we both watched the ball soar and fall to earth. "But you're still, um, *partially* radical?"

She whopped another ball and spoke while following its flight. "Partially, yes."

"You were pretty radical when we played the golf match."

"You brought out my competitive side." She leaned down and grabbed her bucket of golf balls and handed it to me. "Go ahead, take half of these, and we'll have a little rematch."

Somehow I knew this might happen. I poured out half the balls onto a mat and gave her back the bucket. Then I stretched for a moment and took a few practice swings with my 5-iron. "Hit the 100-yard sign?" I asked. "What's the bet?"

"A quarter per hit," she said, rolling her first ball into position on her mat. "Loser pays immediately."

With just the two of us out there and no supporters on either side, the little wager became a kind of good-natured competition. Twenty minutes later, after all the balls were struck, I had hit the sign three times, and Lin had hit it twice.

With a shrug and a hint of a smile, she slung her golf bag over her shoulder, reached into her pocket, and handed me a quarter. "You got talent, Mr. Hackett. I'll see ya around."

I stuffed the coin in my own pocket and watched as she walked back toward the shop and the parking lot. When she was some ten mats away, she turned and raised her voice. "By the way, Chris, your Super Blaster story was silly."

"But it made you laugh, didn't it?"

"Maybe once." She loped on toward the lot but spoke over her shoulder and golf bag. "Okay, maybe twice."

I remained out on the range, picking up empty buckets and pieces of blown trash, all the while thinking how strange this day had become, and how I suddenly felt a little more at peace with the world.

The feeling did not last long.

At closing time Cack came in to the shop with the day's mail, which we'd both forgotten to check at lunchtime. The small white envelope on top of the stack looked like some kind of invitation, though there was no return address. I opened it to find anything but an invite. On a 3 x 5 card was scrawled a note:

You had best cease entertaining Republicans and encouraging them to hit golf balls like bullets. They've already wasted enough money on wars and their self-serving agendas. Better watch your back, boy!
—Very worried 'bout you

I crumpled this one just like its predecessor and tossed it into the trash. I didn't bother to tell Cack about it. You've seen one extremist, you've seen 'em all.

13

LESSON FOR TODAY

**All players must respect the game, its
rules and traditions—even if one of
the traditions is that dignitaries get
preferred tee times.**

She phoned me from a TV station lobby in Montgomery,
Alabama. "Chris, I plugged your range to a person of influence.
Be expecting a surprise."

It was 7:15 a.m. when Molly called. I lay on the couch in
the den of my small suburban house, feet propped on pillows,
the sports page doubling as a blanket. I had fallen asleep here
while watching the news, and it took me a minute to awaken
fully. "Mornin', Molly. Is this person publicity related or sports
related?" I paused to think of more options, though mostly I
was thinking of a good breakfast. "Or both...or neither?"

"Kinda sports related," she said. Even at this early hour,
Molly's phone voice was verbal honey; no wonder they put her
on television. Then she added, "And with good possibilities for
increased publicity."

"You're being evasive," I chided.

"I'm a woman in politics. It's my nature to be evasive."

My yawn had nothing to do with her. I was a multiyawn per morning guy, and one who welcomed Molly's call no matter the time of day. "The publicity you've already sent is still paying off. Last night I had fifty more liberals whacking balls at the conservative jester."

"Cack?" she asked.

"Nope, I did it myself. But my customers said I wasn't as funny, that they wanted to be insulted by Cack or not be insulted at all. Anyway, within an hour I sold another four hundred dollars worth of golf balls."

"That should keep syrup on your plate."

"Speaking of, when can we—"

"Chris, I'm sorry I have to go." Her tone had changed from casual to hurried. "The makeup person needs to prep me for this interview. Let's talk again tonight. Take care."

Before I could even say "bye" she'd hung up.

At 1:45 p.m., three men in dark suits and sunglasses came striding into my pro shop. They had no golf clubs, just serious expressions on their faces. My first thought was they were those cloned Mr. Smiths from the *The Matrix*.

"Is there a Chris Hackett here?" the middle one asked. He nudged his sunglasses down his nose and peered over them.

"I'm…him."

"Sir, would you consent to a head of state stopping by your facility?"

"A head of which state? South Carolina or Georgia?"

The serious man in the suit frowned. "The president, son. The President of the United States is passing through the low country today on a campaign run. He would like to hit a few golf balls on your driving range."

Just now realizing that this guy was Secret Service, I quashed my nerves and blurted, "Would you like me to reserve an hour later this evening? Just for him? I'll be glad to close the range for the president, give him some privacy."

The suit shook his head. "Unless he changes his mind, he'll be here in the next thirty minutes. Can you concur with this arrangement?"

"Um, yes," I stammered. "Hack's Golf Center is thrilled to concur." I didn't even know what I was saying; I was just blabbering words. "Let me tell my groundskeeper to bring up some new golf balls and to clear the range of customers."

Secret Service Man held up his hands in protest. "No. Don't tell the customers to leave. We'll want a crowd around…a publicity thing, you understand. There'll be TV cameras."

The other two suits fanned out across my pro shop, looking through windows at the range, staring up at the roof, at surrounding trees.

Secret Service Man looked me over, head to toe. "Do you keep a gun on the premises, Mr. Hackett? If so, we'll need to confiscate it until the president has departed."

It was the nature of his job, I figured. "No gun in here, sir. Just lots of golf clubs."

He nodded, then came around my counter and peered inside the drawers.

The second suit stepped outside, and through the glass door I saw him speak into a thick walkie-talkie.

I called Cack on my own walkie-talkie, which wasn't nearly as thick or expensive. Ours were purchased at Target, made of purple plastic, and had a range of about three hundred yards. In fact, if Cack toiled at the outer fence picking up range balls near the 315-yard sign, our walkie-talkies wouldn't work. I pressed the talk button and said, "Groundskeeper? Are you there?"

A scratchy tone gave way to clarity. "Yeah, boss?"

"Whatcha doing?"

"Well, at the moment I'm dumping tubs of used golf balls into plastic buckets in order that you and I may present them in an attractive package so that you and I can sell them over and over and thus earn the monies necessary to survive the escalating costs of subsisting in the overpriced city of Charleston."

Sometimes Cack talked like that after he'd consumed too many Mountain Dews—I always blamed it on the sugar in his system. "I mean what are you *really* doin'?"

"Washin' golf balls and trying to come up with more one-liners to tick off Southerners, teenagers, and dumb athletes."

"You'd better change that to Republicans."

"Why, boss?"

"Because I think you're about to have an opportunity to antagonize the president."

A short pause. "The president of Carolina First Bank? I told that guy last week he couldn't swing worth beans. Spends too much time countin' money."

"No, Cack. The President of *the United States.* He'll be here in less than thirty minutes."

Another pause. "I'll need some proof before I fall for this one."

"Step out of the maintenance shed for a second and look toward the pro shop. See those guys in dark suits and sunglasses?"

Ten seconds of silence. Then, "I see 'em."

"They look like golfers to you?"

"No, they look like they're packin' guns under them suits."

"I imagine they are. Now, I need you to put fifty new golf balls in a plastic bucket and set them out on the newest hitting mat. Then start your cart and get ready to annoy the president."

"I can't annoy the *president,* Chris. I voted for the man."

"You can annoy anybody, Cack. Just pretend he's an average hacker."

His sigh was followed by a conciliatory, "Ten-four. But this is mighty spontaneous for a Republican administration."

"I know, but this is how things work in the political world."

"How do you know how things work?" Cack asked with a full dose of sarcasm. "All you've done your entire adult life is teach golf and date your students."

"Molly told me this is how things work."

"Are you two dating?"

"Just get your bullhorn ready."

Sirens preceded police cars, which preceded the first black limo, the second black limo, the third, plus the TV vans and other media who trailed behind. By this time I had e-mailed every Charlestonian who'd signed my guest register, including the atheists, the Bubbas, Tongue Depressuh, the conservative teenagers who did not dress conservatively, even Benny and Pauly Three Seeds, who said if he made it there in time he'd have many questions for the Prez.

Soon a dozen policemen and Secret Service gathered at the door of the third limo. Mere feet away, cameramen jostled for position, anticipation on their faces. People parked in the street and streamed like ants toward my parking lot. Then, just as one of the Secret Service guys reached for the door of the limo, three other SS rushed to the second limo, snatched open the door, and led the president through the crowd. South Carolina Senator DeMint trailed in his wake, followed by, in descending order, the rest of the political food chain.

The scene was surreal—the Prez tromping through my green and white pea gravel toward the glass doors, behind him the cheers tainted by boos, the boos diluted by cheers. He strode right toward my counter, looking confident and upbeat. "Hi there," he said and extended his right hand. "They call me Dubya."

I shook his hand firmly. "And I'm Chris. Chris Hackett." It felt strangely patriotic to grasp the presidential palm. After he let go I pulled from behind the counter my Mizuno 5-iron. "Do you need to borrow a club, sir?"

Presidential fingers wrapped around the grip. He backed from the counter and tested the club, which caused the Secret Service and the media to domino backward behind him. The Prez waggled my club a second time, gave it a nod of satisfaction. "This'll do fine, Chris. Which way to the range?"

I pointed behind me, and just like that, the entourage flowed past. From the parking lot I heard someone yell, "With troops still dying in the Middle East, should you be practicing golf, sir?!"

I wondered what it must be like to be constantly surrounded by a wall of human protection, to have your every sentence, every blunder, recorded on camera. As the entourage made its way through my pro shop and out toward the hitting mats, I felt honored to be host, yet glad that my life was simpler than his. Other than the increased publicity due to Molly's promotional snippet, my job was unencumbered by attention, unspectacular in comparison. Just Cack, myself, some golf balls, and routine maintenance. We liked it this way.

I followed the crowd out behind the hitting mats. Someone nudged me up to the front until I was standing there beside W, who rolled up the sleeves of his blue button-down and turned to the cameras. "Where do y'all want me to aim? The 100-yard marker?" He motioned with my 5-iron toward the marker.

"No, sir," I replied. "Here at Hack's we have *moving* targets."

W looked as confused as W could look. He turned to an aide. "What does he mean . . . *moving* targets?"

The aide pointed past the president and out toward the maintenance shed. Cack came barreling across the Bermuda, a cardboard donkey affixed to our side of the cage, red, white, and blue ribbons fluttering from the top. He circled in front of the president some fifty yards away and raised the bullhorn. "Mister President, I sure hope you're more efficient with that golf club than you were in sending relief to New Or-leens!"

W looked ashen. He gripped my 5-iron and addressed the ball. "That's my moving target?"

An aide leaned in. "Yes, Mister President . . . the golf cart . . . it's moving."

The presidential swing was not bad, although he missed Cack by forty yards. After three more attempts, W looked frustrated.

"Anyone ever hit that guy?" he asked.

"Several people have, sir," I replied, kneeling now so the press corps could shoot over me. "There's a certain technique that seems to work."

He promptly handed me the club. "So how about a quick lesson, Chris?"

Just as I'd done with the teenage girls, I lined up five balls in a row and explained my method. He appeared quite interested.

"Remember, Mr. President," I said as I demonstrated a punch shot, "you are the machine gun; the golf balls are your bullets."

The aide leaned in again. "And pretend that cart is the Taliban, sir."

That comment seemed to inspire W. Well, that and Cack's next insult. Just under a hundred yards away, Cack lifted the bullhorn high and said, "That swing of yours got more loops in it than a giant pretzel. I'm gonna start calling you President Pretzel-swing."

Unused to such put-downs, the Prez took my club back, addressed the four remaining balls on the mat, and fired. He whacked them hard, in quick succession. His fourth shot bounced into the cage and gonged the donkey. *Clang.*

Most of the crowd erupted in cheers. Others booed.

"Luck!" shouted Cack through his bullhorn. "Pure dee luck! As lucky as you winning Ohio in '04!"

W thrust a fist into the air. Then he turned to the cameras. "Did y'all get that shot? Please tell me you got some video of me hitting that loudmouth?"

The press corps said together, "We got it, Mr. President."

Satisfied, Dubya handed me my club, then shook my hand with vigor. "Thank you, Chris. All the best with your business." He spoke quickly, a man rushed for time. "This country's backbone is the entrepreneur, you know."

"Yessir, it's a pleasure to have you here at Hack's."

He spent half a minute shaking hands with the crowd and autographed three golf caps for the teenagers. The festivities were over quickly, however. They were over as soon as that aide had him by the arm. "Mister President, Air Force One is ready at the airport. We need to hurry to make DC by six thirty. You're having dinner with the ambassadors."

W turned and shrugged at us, as if to say, "This is my life."

And just like that, the entourage streamed past my hitting mats and into the pro shop and out into the parking lot. Cack, of course, was waiting for him there. Wearing his Uncle Sam hat and his widest grin, Cack showed the president the very golf ball that had hit the cart and asked him to auto-graph it.

With a red Sharpie that Cack offered, W signed the ball, shook his hand, and hurried out to the line of waiting limos. This time he disappeared into the third one.

The motorcade sped away, and as they did, the same protes-tor shouted again, "When troops are still dying in the Middle East, sir, why would you practice golf?!"

Yes, I liked my simple life.

Cack and I spent the better part of the afternoon in the pro shop, talking about the visit and wondering if Molly had really suggested the stopover. We speculated on whether she'd ever even met the president or if this was all just blind luck. The six o' clock news gave a brief mention of the event, and while the weather report ran, I began closing procedures. It had been a slow revenue day, disappointing considering what had occurred.

But then Cack came around the counter and pulled from the upper pocket of his overalls what looked like a check. "Boss, I've been saving this for a surprise. One of those aides gave me this to give you."

He handed me a check from the U.S. Treasury. It was made out to Hack's in the sum of $200.00.

"For renting out your range for ten minutes," Cack said and tapped a dirty finger on the amount. "At least that's what the guy told me."

I admired the check for a moment before tucking it into the register. "Our tax dollars at work, Cackster. Not bad."

He looked pleased when I reached into the register and tipped him half the total.

At sunset, some five hours after the surprise presidential visit, a dozen seagulls gathered on the far end of the range. At first they appeared to be lingering spectators, still hanging around after a celebrity's departure. But soon one of the gulls waddled out onto the grass and picked up a golf ball in its beak. He attempted to fly with it, but dropped the ball soon after taking flight. Like a contest of who could fly the farthest with stolen goods, this looked to be a game instead of petty thievery. And to my surprise, the birds appeared to take turns, squawking as if they all agreed on the rules.

One portly gull snatched a ball in its beak and rose more than fifty feet in the air before dropping the ball back to the grass. In seconds another swooped down and did the exact same thing. But then Cack emerged from the maintenance shed, ran out onto the range, and threw a full can of Mountain Dew at the gathering. The carbonated blast scared the gulls away—except for the fat one, who continued to try its best to advance the ball farther.

I, too, needed to advance the ball farther, and so before I closed the shop I typed a quick e-mail to my favorite student:

M

*You'll never guess **Who** stopped by today.*
What do I owe you? (And when can I pay up?!)
    —C

14

LESSON FOR TODAY

Flameouts can occur anywhere: on the course, off the course, and sometimes *to* the course.

My cash register lay burned and smashed in the pea gravel. It was 1:02 a.m. when I got the call; 1:08 when I arrived at my range and saw my golf shop in flames, the front wall toppled over into the parking lot.

Sirens blared over one another, so loud I could not think. Smoke swirled and rose into the night. Firemen ran to and fro, emergency lights flashing in streaks of red and yellow. At first I could not even leave my truck. It was as if my mind had shut down, too stimulated to function. Somehow I opened my door and stumbled out, fixated on a flashing light reflecting off what used to be my pro shop. I stood teetering, one hand on the hood, one knee ramming a front tire as I mouthed, "No no no!"

Seconds later I stumbled forward, toward flames that stubbornly leapt into the night sky.

A stocky fireman, weighed down with a fire hose, brushed by me and shouted, "Stay back, sir!"

The impulse to save things gave way to anger. I looked every direction for someone to blame. Out of options, I looked sky-ward and blamed God. *This is what I get for busting my tail to please customers?*

Three more firefighters ran by me. I backed against my truck and collapsed across the hood, one side of my face hot from the metal, the other from the seared air. If tears fell, they imme-diately dried in the heat. All I could do was watch plumes of high-pressure water spew from two fire trucks.

A minute later my sign fell off the building. It had burned through on one side and toppled forward into the parking lot.

A third and fourth fire hose slithered across the asphalt and blasted twin arcs of water upon the blaze. For long minutes flames ate water. For longer minutes fire and water fought to a draw before fire finally succumbed.

Now a wet, smoky stench engulfed us all. Again I moved toward the remains. An older man rushed over to me. He wore civilian clothes but identified himself as the arson inspector.

"Who did this?" I demanded.

He said nothing.

Instead he led me over to the east side of the parking lot and pointed ahead of us. On the sidewalk that led to the pea gravel, spray painted in what looked like blue paint, were words that hollowed my soul: **Bias goes up in flames!!**

The inspector knelt and touched the dried paint. "It's male handwriting," he said. His index finger traced through the "B" in "Bias."

I knelt beside him, desperate to find out who did it and make someone pay. "You can actually *know* that? From a three-foot, spray-painted 'B' you can know an arsonist is male?"

He wiped his finger with a handkerchief. "Well, I believe whoever spray painted these words is male—the majority of arsonists are men. But he could have had friends, so I'm not saying there weren't females involved. This was planned and executed well."

I watched firemen swing axes into what was left of the back wall until it too lay flat and was in no danger of falling in on anybody. A brief wind blew the smoke eastward, and everyone without a mask took deep breaths and heaved for more.

Sometime in the night—I had no idea when—I called Cack at home. All I got was his voice mail, and all I said was, "Someone torched our business. Get over here."

Weary firemen doused the embers, and soon the winds subsided and the smell of smoke and wet wood dominated once again. The inspector—a hyperactive sort who had circled around the site at least five times—called me over to the west end of the building. He'd found fourteen plastic gas containers melted in the debris. They looked like red clumps of lava that had oozed up from below ground.

"This was planned and executed with precision," he said out of the corner of his mouth. He knelt again and poked at blackened rubble. "Look at how the gas cans were spaced…at even intervals around your building."

My mouth would not form words. Finally I managed to blurt, "Who? Who would do this?"

He pursed his lips, wiped his forehead, but he did not answer my question.

I had not even been to the maintenance shed yet. In the distance I could see that it too had been torched.

"This is a hate crime, son," said the inspector, standing now, hands on hips. He scanned from one end of the building to the other. Then he walked over and read the spray paint on the sidewalk for a second time. "Yep," he said, a look of disgust on his face, "lots of hate in this world."

Time seem suspended, yet before I knew it the sun rose over

what had yesterday been my livelihood. My mouth was dry and my eyes stung. I'd been searching for clues all night. Now sweaty and smelly and covered in ash, I found small solace in the Bermuda grass, uninjured by the attack and shiny with dew. Beyond it the gulls had returned, lining up one by one on my fence and gabbing away, as if debating what had gone wrong.

Sometime before 7:00 a.m. Mr. Vignatti pulled into the parking lot in his gray Volvo. He climbed out of his car, a look of disbelief on his face. For a long minute he stared at the charred wood. Then he went over and read the blue words spray painted on the sidewalk.

I stood some twenty feet away, kicking at the rubble and wondering what he would say to me. But he spoke to the rubble instead. "This…this politics and rage…this is a bad, bad thing."

Shaking his head in slow bouts of disappointment, Mr. Vignatti got into his Volvo and drove away. He never even acknowledged my presence.

15

LESSON FOR TODAY

CSI **plus three friends do not a crime-solving team make.**

Pauly Three Seeds said the liberals did it. Benny insisted it was the conservatives. And Cack, well, he waffled between those choices and one of the atheists, who Cack said became quite angry on the range when referred to as a godless hacker. That incident was a week earlier, however, and on this ashy morning every one of our guesses felt inconclusive, more reaction than wisdom.

In what was left of Hack's parking lot, these three friends stood outside my driver's side window, alternately commenting on the scope of the destruction, offering sympathy, and speculating on who did it. The arson inspector had just left, and the four of us now gazed alone at my piece of scorched earth.

Cack turned from my truck to stare at the smoke still seeping from the rubble. "Makes a man wanna take revenge, don't it?"

Benny chimed in. "Makes me want to sit on somebody."

We all looked at Pauly to hear his version of a threat, but

instead he pulled a pen from his pocket and scrawled something on a business card. Pauly said, "At least it's a start, Chris," and handed me his card. What he'd written on the back only affirmed what I'd already noticed:

The "B" in "Bias" has a long tail on it.

Soon Pauly and Benny had to rush back to their jobs, so I thanked them for the support and told them I'd let them know if any more great clues surfaced.

Cack asked me to wait in the truck while he went to check out his favorite toy. Around the smoldering remains of the pro shop he made his way down to the maintenance shed. I knew what he would find there; I'd already seen it.

He returned minutes later, head down. "Melted the cart, Chris." He looked despondent, overwhelmed. "Maybe the cage is salvageable."

Though my head was not currently programmed for sympathy, I did my best. "I'm sorry, man. I know how much time you put into building it."

"But that's not the worst of it." He pursed his lips, and tears formed in his eyes. "They spray painted 'Hate-Monger' on its side."

This angered me to no end. Cack was the least hate-filled person I knew. He was fun-loving and gracious and customer-friendly. Caught up in silent aggravation, I could not think of what to say to comfort him. He climbed into his own truck, lowered his window, and muttered that he was going home to tell his wife what happened.

He drove away slowly, and for the first time I was left alone to face the consequences. For long minutes I scanned the destruction and ignored the growl in my stomach—I had not eaten a thing since arriving on the scene more than nine hours earlier.

My mind raced through possible suspects. First, of course, were the anticonservatives, the Bush-haters. Then again, this was the pro-Republican South, so the liberal-haters seemed just as likely. But then I thought about the local gangs, kids so bored they had nothing better to do than react with violence when one high school mocked another on my range. Perhaps some Bubbas hated my entertaining the hip-hop guys. Maybe the hip-hop guys hated my welcoming Bubbas. Possibilities swarmed in my head in bee-like flights of speculation. Like the inspector said, lots of hate in this world.

Confusion multiplied by the minute. Thoughts of vindictive rage rose within me. But soon that settled back into something more rational, and I decided to call the person whose suggestions had perhaps led to the crime. I called Molly.

What I thought I wanted to hear was perhaps a little remorse for helping to turn my range into an arena for political venting. That, and perhaps some feminine sympathy. I supposed if I were the sentimental, artsy type, I'd have preceded the call by writing in my journal something like, "She'd come into my life like an unexpected raindrop on a blue-sky day—and she left me with the aftermath of an election-year inferno." But I was neither a journaler nor artsy nor sentimental. My thoughts on the matter were uncomplicated: Why hadn't the two of us considered the possible consequences?

She answered on the third ring.

I dismissed pleasantries and got right to the subject. "Molly, some person or persons set fire to Hack's and spray painted 'Bias goes up in flames' on my sidewalk. My golf shop is destroyed."

A deep inhale, followed by silence. Then, "Oh no, Chris . . . I am sooo sorry. Was anyone hurt?"

"No, it happened after midnight."

"Do they know who did it?"

"Nope."

"Are you furious at me for suggesting that you—"

"Not exactly." I stopped there, battling the impulse to cast partial blame her way. Practicing forgiveness did not come as naturally as practicing my golf swing. And yet the blame really fell on me—and she needed to know that. "Hey, I was the one who agreed to run with that suggestion."

Molly sighed, and I couldn't quite determine if it was from relief or sympathy. Probably some of both. "Chris," she said, "again I am sooo sorry. And I hate to cut this call short, but I'm with senior campaign officials and they're waiting for me."

"It's okay. I really just wanted to hear your voice."

She spoke quickly. "Let me know what I can do. And listen, I have some days off coming up. I'll drive down and help you solve the crime. I'm good at that stuff. I've been watching *CSI* reruns at night in my hotel room."

I managed a brief smile and told her I welcomed all the help I could get. "Our best clue so far is the tail on the letter 'B' in the word 'Bias.'"

She paused as if in deep thought. "Does the B have a curving flippy tail like the curl in a woman's hair? Or is it more of a straight tail with not much curve, like the bottom of a man's tux?"

"The second one."

"Then it's probably a man's handwriting."

"We figured that out already, Mol."

She said she had to run and interview a senator, so we agreed to talk again when we could. After we said good-bye I drove to a nearby Wendy's and ate lunch in my truck, my feet restless in the floorboard, my hands shaking as I ate my sandwich. Being a victim had fostered in me an extreme amount of energy, a conviction that I had to *do* something.

I returned to what remained of Hack's and spent another half hour tromping around the debris, kicking at boards and scattering ash. Down at the maintenance shed I noted the melted cart, the ruined John Deere riding mower. What a waste of good equipment.

I wanted answers—and fast. Cell to ear, I called the arson investigator and demanded an update. He asked me to please be patient. "I'm good at my job, Chris," he said, "but I'm not *same-day* good."

It was now 2:30 p.m., and while the rest of Charleston went about their daily routines I scanned the acreage and swallowed the emptiness of it all. I missed my customers. I missed the old hackers, the young hackers, the too-loud teenagers, the rich women who tipped well, like Mrs. Dupree. I even missed feeling envious of the young fathers who taught their youngsters on my hitting mats. But I was not going to go home and sulk. And I was certainly not going to stand in the middle of the debris and cry. I had to do something, expend the energy. And the only thing that appealed to me came in the form of an old push mower that had survived the blaze.

I grabbed its handle and pulled the mower out onto the grass. Then I looked from fence to fence and wondered how long it would take a man to mow all that—an entire golf range—with just a push mower. Cack and I had never tried, never wanted to. But today I felt determined. Some folks might pout after a personal disaster, and some might become vigilantes. I, however, would mow.

My check of the fuel revealed the push mower was out of

gas. My check of the shed revealed the melted remains of my two gas cans. The arsonist had apparently used my own cans to torch the shed.

I rushed over to Lowe's and found that they were out of five-gallon containers, so instead of two of those I bought five of the smaller, two-gallon variety.

Across the street at a convenience store I swiped my debit card in the pay-at-the-pump slot and pulled the gas nozzle over into my pickup bed.

Perhaps I was in denial, viewing this task of mowing the range as way too important. Still, such labor would help me move forward, stay active and involved instead of dwelling on the limbo of my financial future.

The first two containers filled quickly, efficiently. Midway through the third, I lost my balance and spilled gas in the truck.

Anxious to finish and get to work, I climbed out of the bed and grabbed some paper towels from a dispenser. My blunder went unnoticed, however—except for the store clerk, who kept glancing out the window at me.

I had just filled the fifth container when a patrol car pulled into the lot, circled around the pumps twice, and eased in behind me. There I was, squatting in the bed of my pickup, a victim with five gas cans at his feet. I waved at the officer. He did not wave back.

I figured perhaps the officer was there to fill up his squad car.

Perhaps I was too optimistic.

He was out of the squad car and beside the truck before I could even twist the cap onto the last container.

"Mr. Hackett," he said and peered over into the bed,

"you're going to need to explain why you're carrying around these gas containers...just hours after your business went up in flames."

He gazed upon my inventory and frowned his disgust, though he lacked the patented head shake of the Cackster.

"You know about my business?" I asked, pointing with the gas nozzle in the direction of Hack's.

Foregoing reply, he reached into the truck bed, lifted a container, and sat it back down, as if testing its heft. "The arson investigator is a friend of mine. Said he didn't think you were the type to take revenge, that you'd avoid taking the law into your own hands." He pointed again at the containers. "Wanna explain what you're about to do with these?"

I looked past him and pointed across the street, at empty lots in a suburban development, all of them marked with little orange flags. "Sir, my range is larger than ten of those lots put together, and so I needed a lot of gas. I was simply going back to Hack's to mow, to expend some energy and some pent-up frustration."

"Right, son. And I costarred in *Miami Vice*."

He reached for my arm, and I figured my best bet was not to resist. I could explain myself. After all, I was a victim.

They held me on suspicion of suspicious behavior, or some such charge. Inside police headquarters they led me into an interrogation room and sat me across the table and told me I had better tell the truth. I pleaded my case with passionate voice. "I was just going to mow my driving range, man!"

The interrogating officer nodded as if he'd heard it all before. "Your range is quite large, Mr. Hackett. Don't you always mow it with a riding mower?"

"Yessir, I do. But the riding mower was destroyed in the blaze."

"So now you want us to believe that you intended to mow that entire range with just a push mower?"

The tone of his voice grated against my innocence. "That was my intent, sir."

"Have you ever mowed it with a push mower before?"

"No, I have not."

His blank stare broadcast his doubt. "Mr. Hackett, you had five full gas containers in the back of your truck."

I made a fist but stopped just short of pounding the table. "Yes, but I just wanted to do something physical, and I needed a lot of gas. I wasn't going to torch anything…I mean, I wouldn't even know where to go, or who to go after. All we know so far is that the 'B' in 'Bias' has a long tail on it and that it was likely written by a man. Even Molly agrees."

He exchanged a glance with his cohort. "And who is this Molly?"

"She's a political correspondent. We date a bit."

"Whatever you say, Mr. Hackett."

"Sir, I am not a violent man. And besides, it's only a burned up golf shop. No one got hurt."

His doubting, blank stare nullified my pleading, let-me-go stare. "Mr. Hackett, what you say might or might not be fact, so we've decided to hold you until all this checks out."

Accommodations, of course, were poor. The cell reeked, the bottled water was lukewarm, and the next cell housed a pair of drunks who spent the entire evening debating the pros and cons of Coors Light.

Several questions the cops asked me suggested that I might have torched my own range to get insurance money—which was a total lie. Business had never been better. And my insurance was not that good.

Still, when they allowed me a phone call, I knew whose number to dial.

I called Allstate.

16

LESSON FOR TODAY

As with many a struggling marriage, often-
times the game's most challenging aspect
is getting a grip on finances—regardless of
who controls the checkbook.

Jerry Schooler was not only my Allstate agent, he was perhaps
the best golfer in Charleston. Twice he'd won the city championship, and local legend held that he had once shot a sixty-
five while using just six clubs—less than half of the fourteen
allowed.

Today, however, I had a cop and a desk clerk watching me
make a phone call, so I wanted to talk only about deductibles
and the value of my building.

"Chris, I'm really sorry to hear about your golf shop," Jerry
said as he checked the particulars of my policy. "How's the wife
and kids?"

"I'm *single,* Jerry, remember? But as for the fire, the investiga-
tors still don't know who did it."

"Any ideas yourself?"

"I have ideas. Right now I just need to get out of confinement."

I wasn't sure how much to tell Jerry, though after a moment of silent waffling I forged ahead. "The cops thought I was going to commit a revenge torching."

Long, wary, insurance-agent pause. "So...were ya?"

"No, of course not."

Without giving a reason, Jerry put me on hold. One minute became two, and two, four. Perhaps the phrase "revenge torching" had scared him, and now he was cancelling my policy.

When he came back on the line, I told him this was my only phone call and to please not cut me off. The cop and the desk clerk both watched me without expression. I wondered if my call came with a time limit.

"Chris," Jerry said with calm professionalism, "you'll need to file a police report, and then I'll need you to total the contents inside your golf shop—item by item. If you can put it all in a spreadsheet for us, that would be best."

"Even the three thousand melted golf balls?"

"Even those. Plus any clubs, golf bags, personal possessions, electronics, etcetera. You told me once that you'd videotaped the contents in your building, so if you have that tape it'll be a huge help to us."

I turned my back to the eavesdropping desk clerk and the cop, whose ears had perked up when I mentioned the word "melted." *I cannot believe they suspect me.*

"Jerry, I have the video at home and will be glad to get that for ya, but it may take me a while, since I don't know how long they're going to keep me here. I *am* innocent, ya know."

"Soon as possible," he said, urgency in his tone. "Meanwhile I'll get a claims adjuster out to inspect your building. And hey, when all this settles out, let's get together and play some golf."

I said sure—though I did not want to even think about the sport—and forced a smile at the officer assigned to watch me. He did not smile back; he just came over and took the phone away and escorted me back to the holding cell. After he shut the door he informed me that I'd exceeded my phone minutes.

"No free nights and weekends?" I asked, nose between the bars. "No text messaging?"

"No free Starbucks, either," he mumbled as he walked away.

Early the next morning they let me go.

It was 7:00 a.m., and a policewoman came and unlocked my cell. Without comment she escorted me to the front desk and pointed at a form on the counter. "Read it; sign it."

I read it, signed it. But I didn't appreciate her talking to me as if I were an average Friday night nutcase, being let go after sleeping off a good drunk.

"Mr. Hackett, since your record is clean, and you haven't committed an actual crime...*yet*...we're going to make a deal with you."

I raised my right hand. "I swear, officer, that I was just going to mow my grass and that I was never going to set a fire in revenge."

She looked me up and down, like she didn't trust me. "The deal is, you get to go free if you'll do what you said you were going to do—mow your range with the push mower."

I glanced outside at the sun shining on the parking lot. I had only been locked up for twelve hours, but already I missed the sun. "That's it? That's the deal?"

She motioned to another officer standing out in the lobby. "Officer Cavin will escort you back to your truck."

Officer Cavin was a burly man—my estimate was six-four and two hundred fifty pounds. He followed me out to the parking lot and told me he hoped my free stay in the slammer had me feeling energetic.

I drove across town with my load of gas containers, Officer Cavin right on my tail. We arrived at Hack's and parked at the edge of the property, next to Roycroft's Nursery, which today looked even greener beside the smoldering remains of my pro shop. The contrast was vivid—to the left of me sat ruins, to the right stood some six-feet-tall yellow flowers. Mr. Roycroft had labeled them "swamp sunflowers," and they swayed merrily in the breeze, showing off their botanical happy faces during a week that, for me at least, had proven most unhappy.

I climbed from my truck, turned to Officer Cavin, and raised both arms. "Well, is this all an innocent man has to do to earn back his freedom? Just go mow what I had intended to mow in the first place?"

At first he just nodded and watched me unload the gas containers. I noticed too that he preferred munching raw carrots to devouring donuts. I had three gas containers in hand and was headed for the maintenance shed when he lowered his window and summoned me to his squad car.

I hurried over and arrived panting. "Sir?"

He turned down his radio, which was tuned not to police band but to a University of South Carolina football talk show. Then he rested his left arm in the window and raised a finger to me. "Mr. Hackett, law enforcement is doing everything it can to find out which person or persons committed the arson. Do not, and I stress *do not*, think about taking the law into your own hands. Understand?"

I wanted to shout my innocence to him—shout it loud and clear, loud enough for all of Charleston to hear—but I didn't think it would do any good so I just nodded and said, "I understand."

He unwrapped some celery sticks and used one to emphasize his point. I was hoping he'd offer it to me, but no such luck. "Stick to rebuilding your business, Mr. Hackett. You had a good thing going when you were teaching and not getting all political."

I stepped back, surprised at his knowledge of me. "You've been to my range?"

He nodded. "My son enrolled in your junior clinic last summer."

And with that he drove away, both hands on the wheel, the celery stalk clutched in his teeth.

I filled the mower with gas and cranked it on the second try. The raw indignity of being falsely suspected lent me even more energy than I'd felt the previous day. With gritted teeth I pushed the mower, and although each pass from teeing area to boundary fence took long minutes to complete, the monotony of the task gave me time to think about rebuilding, to ponder who did it, and also to reflect on Molly. She had offered to accept blame—and that was an impressive gesture.

Two hours passed quickly, but only one quarter of the range had been mowed. Drenched in sweat, I paused at the boundary fence and called Molly on my cell.

She answered with, "Chris! I'm one minute from going into a press conference. How are you and what are you doing?"

"Mowing my range with a push mower. Probably the dumbest thing I've ever done. I'm estimating this'll take over seven hours, and that's if I don't pass out."

"I hope you don't pass out when I tell you my news. I have three days off so I'm coming back to Charleston Friday to help you find who did it and to help you rebuild."

"You really don't have to do that, Mol, but—"

"No arguments. See you Friday."

No doubt she was the busiest woman I'd ever pursued. I was glad knowing of her return, but any romantic thoughts seemed squashed by a new thought orbiting in my head—*could my neighbor be the arsonist?* As I trudged the length of the range again and again, pushing the mower and soaking my T-shirt with sweat, I kept looking over at Mr. Roycroft's thriving nursery and wondering if he should be a suspect, that perhaps he wanted my land to expand his business. But I just could not fathom that such a mild-mannered guy would commit such a crime.

I dismissed the thought completely a few minutes later when he came rumbling across my range on a brand new Toro riding mower. He sold that brand at his nursery, and this one still had the price tag dangling from the steering wheel.

He pulled up and waited for me near the 150-yard marker. "Chris, use this for today, will ya?" He shouted over its engine noise. "You're gonna kill yourself pushing that thing."

He climbed off, and I thanked him as I swung one leg over the seat and mounted the idling Toro. He hustled back to his nursery, and I mentally crossed him off the suspect list and chastised myself for even considering him. *Definitely not Mr. Roycroft.*

When I finished, I returned the mower to him and filled its tank with the remainder of the gas I'd purchased. The smell of burnt wood beckoned me, however, so I excused myself from chitchat and walked over to what remained of Hack's Golf Learning Center. There I kicked again at charred plywood and various piles of ash and debris. I found one of my old PING putters in the rubble, its grip melted, its shaft blackened. The bronze head of the club still looked usable, however, so I went and set the thing in the back of my truck.

I spent the next hour sifting through the mess, all the while juggling two desires: finding anything salvageable and searching for more clues that might point to who did it.

Around the back of the pile I reached the place where the door to my range had stood. Visions of customers coming and going through that door fought with fresh memories of Cack riding back and forth across the Bermuda in his caged cart, taunting the clientele. Where had those good days gone?

In an effort to avoid self-pity, I lifted a section of Sheetrock and peered beneath it. The burned cash register lay on its side. After disposing of the Sheetrock I managed to pry open the drawer of the register. Of course the drawer was empty; whoever did this had even taken the coins—dimes, nickels, pennies, all of it.

A new wave of frustration welled up, a fluid combination consisting of cops suspecting me, fire ruining me, and the audacity of someone stealing even a man's coinage. Suddenly I wanted to break something, something big. So I leaned down and raised the Sheetrock again. But before I slammed it against the ground I noticed a gaping hole in the middle, where a fireman's axe had busted through. With the Sheetrock held in front of me, I peered through the hole and saw something unexpected: no startling evidence, just Mr. Vignatti's gray Volvo pulling into my parking lot.

Mr. V got out slowly, clearly not looking forward to what he was going to say to me.

He called it a very bad thing.

According to Mr. Vignatti, the clause in section 14B of our lease agreement stated that I, the leasee, shall not engage in any action that promotes or encourages protests, social upheaval, criminal behavior, or conduct unbecoming of a golf professional. This clause was included on the day I signed the lease, and I had never thought twice about it.

Mr. Vignatti held great pride in his reputation as a businessman, however, and he'd definitely thought twice about it. He had thought about it so much that he asked me to leave the rubble pile at Hack's and follow him to his office. "Chris," he said, climbing back into his car, "we need to have a talk."

Ten minutes later we sat at opposing ends of his rectangular conference table, this time without including Mr. Roycroft.

Mr. Vignatti gazed at my file for long moments. "Chris," he said, "I am sad to get to this point. I am sad in my heart because you impressed me as good at the teaching of golf."

I knew where this was headed, and I was determined to halt it before it got there. "But Mr. V, please understand that it was not my idea to—"

He pulled a section of newspaper from my file. "Look at this article from the newspaper. It says, 'A golf property leased from local businessman George Vignatti was set ablaze Monday night. According to authorities, the attack may have been fueled by claims of politically biased activities on the part of the leasee of the property, golf instructor Christopher Hackett.'"

I stood and gripped the edge of his table. "But Mr. V, I never showed bias toward any group. Sure, I vote conservative and pro-business, but the range stuff was all in the name of fun. I let liberals bash conservatives and the conservatives bash the liberals...and the atheists bashed religious folks. There was never any *bias* toward anyone."

He put a finger to his mustache and stroked the outer hairs. "Did you encourage religious folks to bash atheists too?"

I sat again, figuring a less aggressive posture would serve me well. "They refused on the grounds that it was a bad witness to whack golf balls at pagans...but I did make the offer."

Mr. V shook his Italian head with great disdain. "I am sorry, Chris, but I must protect the Vignatti name. If you are to continue in the golf business, you'll have to find other land to lease."

I slumped in my chair but never broke his gaze. "You cannot do this to me."

He rose from his chair, tucked his files under his left arm. "I'm sorry."

17

LESSON FOR TODAY

Sometimes we just need to be alone for a while.

Marsh grass brushed against my johnboat, faded clusters bending against the port side and releasing off the stern. One more push with the paddle and the little boat and I resumed our drift, at the mercy of an outbound tide pulling us through the inlets of the Cape Romain National Wildlife Refuge.

I had to get away—from everything. If only for a day, or perhaps half a day, I sought uncrowded and undeveloped space in which to think and consider. And now, thirty miles northeast of Charleston, armed with a coastal map borrowed from Cack, I'd found such a place. I had been near these waters before—as a passenger, though, never as captain. As soon as I'd cut my outboard engine and set to drift, the salt air and rippling water confirmed that this was the spot.

The tidal creek wound left and then right, a true serpentine of discovery. *No one out here but me.* In the front of the boat lay an extra life jacket, one I would have offered to Molly except for the fact that she would not arrive until Friday.

What I was looking for was some peace. That, and perhaps a

few native birds. Earlier in the morning, before I'd hitched the johnboat to my truck, I read God's boast about how he does such a good job of feeding and caring for birds that I shouldn't worry about my own life.

I was plenty worried.

So, while I paddled along in pursuit of peace, I figured I might as well use the opportunity to check up on God's dependability: If he really cared for Chris Hackett more than birds, I wanted a basis for comparison—and not from a bunch of city-park pigeons. Seemed to me that city birds had it easy—plenty of feeders and sidewalks and seafood processing plants from which to scrounge up the daily meal. But I sought evidence from the wilder side, from birds that lived in the marsh and subsisted apart from man. Birds that were, like myself, entrepreneurs.

I steered the johnboat into the stronger currents and drifted left around another bend. Out of nowhere a pair of sandpipers zipped past, so fast that I had no time to tell if they were well-fed or malnourished.

"Well, does he?!" I shouted after them. "Does he really take care of you even when the hurricanes blow your habitat to smithereens?"

I drifted on, feeling silly for shouting at sandpipers. Around the next bend, however, much larger and slower specimens appeared in the inlet. Ahead in the glare, they fell from the sky with folded wings and bucket beaks, diving into a school of minnows and bobbing in the aftermath. Over and over they did this, as if they could not quite figure out if this was playtime or feeding hour. The closer I drifted, the more they appeared to smile. Oddly, they seemed not to mind a stranger invading their feast. A fishy smell arose, and beside my boat half-eaten minnows floated in the ripples, so many I could not count them. Their predators were not normal-sized pelicans but fat, overstuffed pelicans, three of them airborne again, eight more waddling on the shore and lumbering into flight, bellies dragging the water until their wings reached full throttle and lifted them skyward.

I watched them come and go, watched them dive and eat and waddle on the shore until the tide slowly changed its mind and covered the sandbar. The feast continued despite the water's reversal, and soon the sight of it all made me hungry.

I pulled my PB and J sandwich from my cooler, unwrapped it, and ate right along with them, swayed toward the opinion that God's boast did indeed apply here in the Carolina low country.

My paddle lay across my lap, and in seconds the tide turned the johnboat northward, back the way I'd come. I'd only been out of the city for a few hours, and yet the break from chaos lent a certain confidence that Hack's could be rebuilt, *somewhere,* regardless of whether the criminal was caught. Sure, I wanted to catch the guy, but not today. This refuge was too serene, too anticatastrophe.

I allowed the currents to push me for long minutes before I started the outboard and cruised back to the landing. It was there, while pulling the boat up on my trailer, that I saw the first fellow human of the day, a man backing his boat down the adjoining ramp. He was an older fellow, obviously a fishing guide, what with the patches on his sleeves and Low Country Expeditions painted on the side of his flatsboat. Yet another entrepreneur.

He backed his boat from his trailer and—since I already had my own secured—I volunteered to hold his tie rope while he went and parked his truck. He smiled, threw the rope to me, and drove up the ramp, twin trails of water dripping off his trailer. Seconds later he jogged back to his boat and thanked me for the assist.

After I tossed him his rope I pointed across the wetlands. "You guide out there?"

"Yep. Four days a week."

"Nice office."

He cranked his very large outboard, turned his cap backward, and took off across the inlet. Over the hum of his engine he shouted, "Beats a gray cubicle any day!"

I could relate. My office of green grass was both a rarity and a blessing—even if I did have to relocate the sod. Still, on the drive back to Charleston I couldn't help but consider all the other ways I could start over. I pondered moves, partnerships, and mergers. I even considered caddying for a college buddy who played on the minitours, the minor leagues of golf.

For a while my thoughts even turned international. I could open up a Hack's of Australia, teach Aussies the finer points of the game. I'd sponsor a summer tournament called the Aboriginal Open, to be played in the outback on all that red dirt. Contestants would use bright yellow golf balls so as not to lose sight of them in the desert, and the holes would be longer than any the golf world had ever seen: each one two miles in length, each a par 12. It would take a player five days to complete the course. You'd tee off on Monday morning and not return until Friday night. This would be half survival test, half golf tournament. Each player would tote a backpack with five liters of water and a pack of granola bars. Winner got ten thousand dollars and a kiss from Miss Australia. Cack, of course, would heckle the players all week from atop a camel.

Ahead on Highway 17 the sun set over the Charleston peninsula. Everything turned orange, and a mile short of the

Cooper River bridge I pulled over to the shoulder—not to watch the sunset but to change into a clean shirt. Best I stayed on this side of the city, since only a half hour remained till tonight's meeting with Golfers of the Roundtable.

Tonight the subject was women, and it was Pauly Three Seeds' turn to lead discussion.

18

LESSON FOR TODAY

A critical skill in golf and relationships is knowing when to ask for help.

Benny reclaimed his spot on Pauly's sofa and sprawled his
massive right arm across its back. "Hack, tonight we're here to
cheer you up. Plus I have advice on how to keep your life on
track."

It was hard to take Benny seriously while he sat there
sporting a T-shirt that read: "Superman Wears Heavy T
Underwear."

"The track is very vague right now, Benny," I muttered. "I
just need to settle my insurance and find new land."

Pauly, in business casual, pulled a kitchen chair into the den
and sat silent for a moment, contemplative as ever. He held a
plate of snacks in his lap and nibbled a grape, then a Dorito,
followed by another grape. "Chris," he said, "would you mind if
I asked you three questions?"

I set my paper plate at my feet and nodded. "As long as they're
brief questions. My mind isn't working so great right now."

He shrugged as if he paid no attention to length, only to
content. "Okay, first question: Who knows best, and I mean
really knows best, how to run your golf business?"

I stared at his floor, a light hardwood with a sprinkling of crumbs. "I do."

I'm glad that was a short question.

"And whose idea was it to allow your range to be used as a political outlet?"

"That would be Molly." *This question too was quite easy and acceptably brief.*

Pauly ate a few more grapes and nodded after each swallow, as if thinking hard on his next question. "Now that it appears some politically sensitive person or persons have torched your business, who suffers the consequences?"

"I do...and Cack." *Three easy answers. Good.*

"What about Molly?" Benny asked.

I knew they'd have a fourth question, probably even a forty-fourth.

The mention of Molly's name riled me to defend her, and I sat up on the edge of my chair. "She made the suggestion, yes. But I ran with the idea, and it's my fault for not considering the possibility of ticking people off. Leave her out of it."

Benny smirked as if he expected my answer. "She just breezes into your life, you let her steer your business, and—"

Frustrated with both of them, I raised a finger of protest. "Excuse me, guys, but she didn't *steer* my business. She made a suggestion."

Pauly placed his hands behind his neck and interlocked his fingers, the confident pose of an interrogator. "Well...why'd you *accept* her suggestion?"

"Because it was good for business."

"The fact that Molly is pretty and personable and single had nothing to do with it?"

I sat back in my chair, crossed my legs. "Maybe a little."

Pauly suppressed a laugh at my admittance. "Well, at least

you can see where you went wrong. Which is more than we can say of Adam."

"Which Adam?" I asked, shocked at how a compartmentalized thinker like Pauly could change subjects so fast. "The passive one in the garden? With Eve?"

Pauly nodded. "Yes, that one. Do you remember what God said to him right off the bat?"

"Of course I know…he told Adam to not eat the fruit."

Here they came, more rapid-fire questions, zooming across his den. "And what did Adam do with this information?"

"I reckon he shared it with Eve…who didn't listen very well."

"So, what did God do then?"

Benny raised his hand. "From what I remember, he came looking for Adam, who was busy inventing the first pair of fig-leaf boxers."

Pauly almost laughed out loud. But before he could summon his next question, I cut him off. "Pauly, if you're trying to create a scenario where you compare me to Adam, it won't work, mainly because I didn't point the finger at Eve, who is really *Molly,* and cast blame on her. And I didn't stand there while some—"

"Talking snake slithered onto your range?"

No, not talking snakes again! Last time I heard an adult mention that snake, I ended up losing a golf match to a feminist.

Benny thumped his plastic cup. "Are you still with us, Chris? You seemed to have zoned out."

"I did. Sort of."

"Do you need to be somewhere else?"

I shook my head no. "Nah, but DC might be nice after the elections."

Regardless of my distracted thoughts and comments, their

inevitable conclusion was that I had failed to weigh the true costs of trying to impress Miss Molly Cusack. According to Benny and Pauly, following her advice had drained me of more money than all of my prior business mistakes, plus all the cash I'd spent on dinner dates in the past ten years combined—and they knew I was not a cheapskate when it came to dinner. "Teach well, eat well" was the motto that had hung in my office at Hack's. I had etched those words into a thin piece of oak, using a wood-burning tool I'd owned since high school. But that motto, too, perished in the blaze.

Before our meeting broke up, Pauly turned an empty paper plate upside down and plucked a pen from his shirt pocket. "Chris, try to follow this for a sec."

He didn't bother to ask me if I wanted to follow whatever it was he was drawing; he just barged ahead. Tonight he was on a roll.

"See this square?" With his pen Pauly drew a blue square, about two inches in width.

"I see it."

"You alone have to decide what is allowed inside your square. I look at my square like this: God owns the entire thing, but the square still has four corners. One corner is for me, one is for my wife, one is for my three little girls, and one is for my career."

Benny leaned forward to check out the drawing. "If you ever put another child in that third corner, we'll have to give you a new nickname."

"Be serious, Benny," Pauly said. "How 'bout your own square?"

Benny tugged at his sock, paused, tugged his other sock. Then he sat back on the sofa. "Well, since we don't have kids yet, I s'pose one corner is my wife, one is career, and the other two corners are both for me...since I'm big like that."

Their attention turned to me, and I muttered something about my square being half melted, what with the fire and all, but I could acknowledge that one corner was for me and one for my career.

Pauly pointed at me with a Dorito. "Does Molly belong in your square?"

I nearly came out of my seat. "We've only been on a few dates, man! I'm not ready for serious stuff like offering her part of my square."

"Offer her a square of dark chocolate then," Benny said. "Women love that stuff."

Benny resembled an overgrown class clown, and I wondered if he was ever serious about anything. I didn't bother to laugh at his comment, probably because I was too focused on myself. I knew it wasn't like me to be uptight around these guys. Then again, I'd never lost in the same week a golf shop, a land lease, and a large chunk of pride.

After comparing the manly view of squares to the women's view—Benny said they don't view life in squares; it's more like one of those giant swirled lollipops where everything runs together—the three of us got up and went into the kitchen for refills and a change of topic. While pouring orange juice over crushed ice, I told them I still had no idea who had set the fire.

"It was that feminist who you played golf against," Benny offered and tore open a second bag of Doritos.

I shook my head. "Nope, don't think so. We sorta made our peace the other day."

Pauly turned from the sink and said, "What about that guy who owns the nursery next to you?"

I shook my head again. "Wrong again, Pauly. Too generous a guy."

We stayed in the kitchen for the rest of the meeting. I kept the topic centered on the arsonist and told them Molly would be here on Friday and the two of us were going to try to figure out who did it.

After Benny expressed his doubts about my crime-solving abilities, he excused himself, saying he had a movie date with his wife and could not be late. I hung around the front steps of Pauly's house because Pauly said he had something to say to me in private.

"You seem so obsessed with this arsonist, Chris," he said in a low, don't-wake-the-kids voice. "Why don't you get away for a couple days? Take a trip somewhere."

I stepped off the bricks onto his sidewalk and offered a negatory head shake. "I can't travel, man. I just lost my business. I have to find some new land and rebuild."

Pauly sighed. "This may sound out of left field, but it might be good to get your mind off things by finding a part-time job, something light and menial."

I told him I'd think about it, and that in the meantime I was working on an idea for how to identify the guilty party. He opened his front door to go inside but turned and said, "One other thing, Chris. You sorta smell like fish tonight. What's up with *that*?"

I remembered tossing a few minnows to the pelicans, but had not detected the scent on my clothes. "Took my johnboat out. To Cape Romain."

Pauly nodded. "Trying to find some peace?"

I waved good night and turned for my truck. "Yep."

He called out, "So, did ya?"

"For an hour or so."

19

LESSON FOR TODAY

**Missing your job is sorta like missing
your sweetheart—the evidence tends
to show up in everything you do.**

Why not?

My attempt to forget my circumstances for a day led me to
the lobby of an independent job placement service. They had
accepted my resume via fax and concluded quickly that I was
not looking for a long-term position.

An assistant manager, no more than twenty-five years of age,
asked me to wait in the lobby. I had never visited a temporary
employment agency before. But I comforted myself with the
knowledge that I was here only to find part-time work, something for next week after Molly left, when I'd likely need to distract myself until the insurance settlement.

Next to the black vinyl sofa I picked up a *People* magazine
and read celebrity opinions on the upcoming elections. The
page was dominated by caustic insults from the Hollywood
elite. It seemed silly, these self-serving members of the A-list
trying to tell me, via that fount of wisdom known as *People,*
how our elected leaders—who are *others*–serving—should govern

the country. That one column made me want to puke almost as bad as seeing my golf shop burn. But not quite.

Soon I exchanged *People* for *Business Weekly* and learned that interest rates on premium money market accounts had risen to 4.25 percent. I applied this rate to the roughly thirty grand that I estimated I'd net from Allstate for my golf shop equity and my equipment. Until I began new work, that would be my income: about a hundred bucks per month in interest.

Just as I flipped a page and grew interested in the after-work rituals of Wall Street's elite, a placement rep stuck his head out from his office and summoned me inside.

We shook hands, and I thanked him for seeing me. I sat opposite his desk in a plastic chair. He held my resume in hand and spoke over the top of it. "Christopher, what have you done besides teach golf?"

"Not a lot. But I have a little bit of writing experience . . . short stories mostly."

For a full minute he thumbed through a stack of job openings. "The only thing I have in a related field is a part-time reviewer for a biweekly arts and music newspaper. This is a very part-time position, no more than three or four hours per week. The paper is one of those ten-page freebies that people pick up at newsstands. They'll pay twenty bucks per review. But you gotta be good."

"What would I review?"

He showed me the hiring requirements at the top of the page. "First assignment is a threesome of new CDs. One's country, one's rap, one's heavy metal."

I sat back in the chair and pondered this for all of four seconds. "Sure, I can handle that. Can I do it next week?"

"No, you'd have to begin today. They have deadlines."

He rose from behind his desk, went to his copy machine, and made me a copy of the instructions. "First you have to write a trial review for each CD. Then it has to be approved by both the paper's manager and its editor." He walked over and handed me my copy. "We can't just assign this job to someone without knowing if they have ability."

"Of course not."

Next he strode into a back office and returned with three CDs, all of them still in their clear plastic packaging. He handed them over. "Go home and listen to these, write a review for each, use no more than one hundred fifty words per review, and have them on my desk within twenty-four hours. Got it?"

"Will do."

Trying to forget all that had gone wrong that week, I drove straight home and spent a few minutes kneeling in front of my stereo, debating which CD to listen to first. Since Molly would be here tomorrow, I had extra incentive to get this done. The top CD in the stack of three was by a group called Momma's Corn-fed Quartet, which I figured was the country CD. The second CD was by Thrilla Chilla Killa, and I guessed correctly that this one was rap. The third utilized some disturbing artwork, apparently a drawing by one of the members of the heavy metal group who had joyfully named themselves Morbid Mummies of Blackness.

I decided to begin with the debut album of Momma's Corn-fed Quartet. Somehow the group consisted of six band members instead of four, which their drummer explained away on the back cover of the CD by stating that their natural gifts lay in the realm of music, not math.

An hour later I had typed my review on my computer and

printed two copies, one for the manager of the job placement service, one for myself in case I needed to build a portfolio of work:

> Momma's Corn-fed Quartet serve up a charbroiled brand of country and bluegrass that is better than Burger King when you're really hungry for a charbroiled burger from a fast-food restaurant that serves charbroiled burgers. Their music soars like a well-struck 3-wood shot from an elevated tee on a downhill golf hole with a spectacular view of the Blue Ridge Mountains. The drummer pounds his drums like a PGA Tour pro pounds practice balls. The singer's voice is smoother than the greens at Augusta National. Overall, I highly recommend this debut album from Momma's Corn-fed Quartet, who surely must eat lots more than corn because their members average over 290 pounds each.
> —Reviewed by Christopher Hackett, September 30

By three o' clock I had typed my review of the debut album from Thrilla Chilla Killa:

> Backbeats and percussion drive the harmonies on singles like "Bust Yo Lip Wif My Heavy Brick Rhymes." However, worn-out ghetto themes boasting of fancy cars and big-bootied women do not distinguish this album from any of the other forty million rap albums that boast of fancy cars and big-bootied women. Listening to this album is kind of like watching a robot hit golf balls over and over, with no difference in the distance or direction the golf ball travels. However, the members of Thrilla Chilla

Killa have great tempo, the kind of tempo that would allow them to become very good golfers should they ever decide to spend some of their money on golf clubs and golf lessons.

—Reviewed by Christopher Hackett, September 30

Making the switch from country to rap and now to heavy metal made me genre dizzy. Nevertheless, I ejected the second CD and replaced it with the one from Morbid Mummies of Blackness. One more to go.

My walls shook as this metal CD played, and by four fifteen I had typed my third review:

Distorted guitars and much yelling by lead singer Vyle Putrid makes it difficult for this listener to under-stand the lyrics. Apparently, Mr. Putrid and his Morbid Mummies band mates are mad at the entire world, even tiny little countries like the Dominican Republic, whose citizens surely have better things to do than figure out mummy lyrics. In fact, understanding the lyrics on this album is as difficult as hitting a golf ball from the deck of the Manhattan Ferry, making it carom once off the Empire State Building, roll down Broadway, hop into the lobby of the Imperial Theatre, and settle into a front row seat for a matinee showing of *Les Miserables*. Over-all, I think Morbid Mummies of Blackness should tone things down a bit, perhaps try playing something slower and softer, like the background music CBS plays during The Masters telecast every April, when the azaleas are in bloom.

—Reviewed by Christopher Hackett, September 30

I ran a spell check and confirmed that the word count did not exceed my limit. In general I felt proud of my reviews, especially the fact that I showed diversity of knowledge by including lines about Dominican Republic and Broadway.

I figured sixty bucks for three hours' work was not the worst job in the world. And perhaps I could grow this into a bigger gig, at least until I found another piece of land to lease. Thus inspired, I returned to the temp agency at 4:45 p.m. and promptly handed over my reviews to the young assistant manager. He excused himself, entered his manager's office, and picked up the phone. Then he closed the door.

I hoped he had called the ten-page freebie paper and gained permission for me to review a dozen more CDs. Perhaps two dozen. I mean, getting to sit in air-conditioning and listen to music and get paid for it was just the kind of break I needed from the stress of the past week.

The agency manager walked out into the lobby, which was empty except for me.

"Your former job was golf instructor, right Mr. Hackett?" he inquired in a tone vaguely reminiscent of my third grade teacher, Mrs. Pennington, queen of condescension.

I gripped my ink pen like a club and made a swinging motion. "Yessir, that's what I do best. Or rather, *did* best until someone torched my business."

He pursed his lips, ran a hand through his buzz cut. "Chris, perhaps you should look for a job in that industry."

I stepped toward him, palms extended. "Aren't my three reviews at least…*publishable*?"

He shook his head no, looked down at the second review, paused, shook his head no a second time, reread the third review, paused again, and shook his head no a third time.

Finally he set the reviews on his desk and just let his arms hang at his sides. Then he squared his shoulders to me, extended his own palms—the posture of complete honesty. "Look, man, just pursue your passion, okay? I've loved the job placement business ever since I graduated from the Citadel. Why don't you just go full bore back into the golf industry?"

Stunned to hear a stranger blurt just what I was thinking, I backed toward the exit. "You can have those reviews. No charge…feel free to use them in case you can't find something better."

He waved his good-bye. "Good luck to you, Mr. Hackett."

Losing a one-day job meant little, but now I also feared losing Cack. He pulled into my driveway Friday morning, rolling slowly toward me as I loaded tools into my pickup bed. I wasn't sure what to say to him. He'd been my only salaried employee, and now there was no way I could offer him anything resembling an income. I had no emergency fund for such matters. No supplemental income for lost wages. I couldn't even give him a promise of when—or if—the business would start anew.

My intent this morning was to go dig through the rubble again. Now Cack had arrived unannounced, though it was good to see him again. I pushed my shovel into the rear of my truck and turned to greet him.

He pointed at the tools and let his gesture suffice as a question.

At his door I said, "Was about to go sift through the debris again…and maybe go look for a new piece of land."

He remained seated in his truck and popped the top off a Lipton tea—an unusual beverage for him. He drank once and turned off his engine. "Land's expensive in these parts."

"I know."

He held his can up and stared at it as if it contained some alien liquid. Without looking up at me he said, "You suspect that man-hatin' woman set the fire?"

Not expecting the question, I shut my eyes, sighed, shook my head. "Nope, I really don't. But I've got an idea how to help the investigator figure out who did it."

He took a long drink of his Lipton. "You and I both know who did it."

"No, Cack, we don't."

His patented head shake was all I needed to see to realize how strongly he disagreed. "Consider this: The Prez is here one day, hamming it up on your range and poking jabs at the liberals, and then the next day someone burns down our shop and paints 'Bias goes up in flames' on our sidewalk. That ain't hard to figure out."

I folded my arms and frowned. "I know what it's like to be falsely accused. I just want a little evidence before I go pointing fingers."

He thumped his forefinger against the tin of his can. Over and over he did this, as if this helped him think. But he wasn't thinking about solving crimes; turned out he was thinking about how to tell me his news. "I got a job offer yesterday."

"Where?" I demanded, not wanting to hear this. "Joey at Yeamans Hall offered you a job?"

He pursed his lips, tapped a finger on his steering wheel. "Yep."

"And you took it?"

"Told him I'd work hourly until I knew if you'd rebuild or not." His expression broadcast a mix of sympathy and duty. "My wife takes medicines, Chris. I gotta have an income."

So did I. After he'd backed out of my driveway and left, I felt an even greater urgency to begin anew. Cack was not only a great employee, he was also a very good friend.

I left my house a minute after he did. En route to sift rubble, I sped to save time. Molly was due in at noon, and together we were going to solve a crime.

20

LESSON FOR TODAY

If a player in a foursome loses his or her golf ball (or a member of a double date loses his or her date), etiquette calls for all playing partners to assist in the search.

Whether gazed at from a distance or up close, Hack's looked ugly. In addition, the whole place smelled like burned wood after it's been watered down and left to rot. Even uglier was the bin full of three thousand golf balls melted in the fire. Like a truck full of candles set ablaze, the outer covers of the golf balls had melted together to form a grotesque patty, black and crusty and reeking of burnt rubber. I kicked the bin twice, just to see if some of the balls would shake loose. But no, they remained stuck, married to the patty.

I knew to avoid self-pity, and yet I also knew that three other golf ranges thrived in the Charleston metro area. All had a working pro shop. None had been the target of political rage. Worse, I was now losing revenue during the busy and prosperous fall months, when the low country air rid itself of humidity and ushered in the first cool whiffs of fall. This was the season, as the Bubbas might say, when "the gettin' was good."

But there was to be no gettin'.

Not that the range was totally unusable—had Mr. Vignatti
not cancelled my lease, I could have set up a temporary building on the range and still used the grass and perhaps half of
the thirty-six hitting mats. At least he'd given me thirty days
to move. Now I felt out of sync with humanity. Here I was
on a Friday morning, picking through ash and splintered
wood while the rest of the work world went about their daily
tasks. The still gray chaos of the scene stung my pride. For
relief I walked out onto the range, where the Bermuda still
drank up the sun and awaited its daily pelting.

Already I missed giving lessons. Already I missed all those
slicers and hookers, hacking away and trying so desperately
to improve. Pauly Three Seeds was right—this was my arena of
competence, and the decisions for how to proceed rested with
no one but me.

I walked the land unhurried, until out near the 100-yard
marker I discovered the arsonist had also used a type of delayed
fuse. He'd poured something—gas, I imagined—onto the middle
of the range, spelling out an insult to punctuate his evil. Four
days had lapsed since the fire, and now, in five-foot letters, the
gasoline had burned the grass and broadcast its message.

Biased Loser!

The arson investigator had said it first—lots o' hate in this
world. More annoyed than angry, I fetched the shovel from the
back of my truck and tromped back out to the grass. Fortunately the grass remained soft from a recent rain, fairly easy to
uproot and flip over. Shovelful by shovelful, I dug up sod and
turned hate facedown in the dirt, where it belonged.

When I finished shoveling, I looked the width and breadth of
the acreage, numbed by the knowledge that this would soon be
someone else's land, that atop this manicured grass would lay
a stranger's business. Perhaps an industrial park. Or perhaps

Mr. Roycroft would expand his nursery. Regardless, I knew I'd just worked my last hour at Hack's—and not for pay either.

I set the shovel over my shoulder and trudged back past the rubble pile, through the pea gravel, and out to the parking lot. I made a fist but stopped short of punching my truck.

Hungry now at 10:00 a.m., I drove down the road to an Atlanta Bread Company and bought an unbuttered bagel— Asiago cheese, lightly toasted. But it had little taste. Not that I was sick, I was just preoccupied with why the arson investigator hadn't called with an update and why Allstate had not called with a settlement offer on the building. Nothing was moving fast enough, nothing except bad stuff, anyway. I kept asking myself why it was that bad stuff comes turbocharged, tires squealing, but good stuff creeps along, its news riding shotgun atop a tortoise shell.

In a corner booth I thumbed through my Day-Timer and called everyone who had scheduled a lesson during the next month and cancelled the lessons. All of the calls were similar in content, though different in tone:

"Yo, Tongue Depressuh. Sorry man, my golf shop burned down. No golf lessons till I get back in business."

Next call. Then another and another. Each one removing future dollars from a wallet that could not afford to lose its dollars, be they future or current.

"Is this Ted Stephens, coach of the Hanahan golf team? Yessir, this is Chris Hackett. I'm afraid I can't host your golf team practices on Tuesday and Thursday afternoons. Hack's is closed…yes, completely gutted."

The hardest calls were to my longtime clients, even though some of them tried their best to distract me from my plight:

"Good afternoon, Mrs. Dupree. How are you?…Yes ma'am, that's a great exercise for improving flexibility.…I guess you heard about Hack's....Four days ago...Yep, it is sad....I don't know when I'll be back, or even where....No ma'am, my lease got cancelled....Yes, it may have been the liberals....I have some insurance, but I don't know how much money I'll get....Your one-brick dog is pregnant?!...The father is a ten-brick dog?...Oh my...No, I've never heard of a long-haired brickette."

I returned to Hack's and found Molly standing in the parking lot beside the rubble pile, her back to me. Excited to see her, I parked next to her rental car, hurried out, and spoke over its roof.

"Not quite what it used to be, right?"

She spun around, met my gaze, and without a word rushed over and hugged me.

"You're early," I said and stepped back to admire her in jeans and a T-shirt. I'd never seen her in such casual clothes. She looked great, and I told her so.

She motioned to the charred debris. "I guess my idea sorta backfired, eh?"

"Our idea, yes." Next I told her about Mr. Vignatti canceling my lease, and she said she felt bad. Then I told her about "Biased Loser" spelled out in the range, and she said she felt worse.

I didn't want this to become a pity party, however, so changing the subject seemed a timely gesture. "How'd you get here so quickly?"

She looked at her watch. "I left Montgomery at five this morning. I wanted to help and to not waste time."

I motioned to her rental car. "Do ya need to check into a hotel first?"

"Did that."

"Hungry?"

"Ate in my car."

I was all ready to buy her lunch, but this was feeling less and less like an appropriate time for a date. So while Molly opened her trunk and exchanged her sandals for a pair of sneakers, I called the arson investigator, faked a calm demeanor, and asked for an update. He surprised me when he told me to stop by, that he had some things to show me. I asked if he'd permit me to bring a friend along, and after a moment of hesitation, he granted my request.

I turned to ask Molly if she wanted to ride with me and smiled when I saw her already seated in my passenger seat.

Those DC women think fast.

21

LESSON FOR TODAY

**Written communication—be it
personal or business related—
is frequently misinterpreted.**

The arson investigator wore a lab coat and escorted us back to
his office, where he'd set up one of those forensic tables, clear-
topped and backlit for examining photographs. He slid onto
its surface an enlarged photo of the spray-painted words from
my sidewalk. **Bias goes up in flames!**

Molly eased in beside him on the left, and I on his right,
peering down at the words but having no idea what to look
for. Nothing in the golf world prepares one to examine crime
scene evidence. And I had major doubts about the political
world.

The investigator's name was Jonathan. He seemed a direct,
no-nonsense type of guy, and he pointed at the B and waited
for us to acknowledge him. "In some cases, spray-painted lettering tends to be similar in style to cursive writing. See the
long tail on the top left of the letter B?"

I leaned closer. "Yeah, we already noticed that. What of it?"

He moved the photo to his left, then slid a second photo

in beside it. Now we had a kind of split-screen view. This new photo read, "Having a Bad Day?"

Together we compared the penmanship. "I see the similar B," I said to him, "but that message wasn't spray-painted at my range."

Jonathan tapped the second photo. "Nope. This one is from a fire last October. On Halloween, in fact. A small office building on the east side of the city burned to the ground. It's still unsolved."

"Was anyone hurt?" Molly asked him.

"No. The fire was started after midnight, just like the one at Hack's."

I tried my best to think like an investigator. Failing at that, I tried my best to imitate an investigator: I traced my index finger over the first B, and Molly did the same with the second. They looked so very similar. And then I thought of the grass at my range, where I'd spotted the words "Biased Loser" burned into the Bermuda.

"Sir," I said, feeling convicted that I should tell him, "there was a third message that you may not know about."

He turned to me, excited. "Where?"

"Apparently the arsonist poured gas onto the grass at my range. It took a few days for the message to burn through, but this morning I found the words 'Biased Loser' in huge letters."

He pulled his car keys from his pocket and shook them. "C'mon, we'll go take a photo."

I grabbed him by the elbow to halt his urgency. "Um, there won't be anything to photograph."

"Why not?"

"Because I had a shovel in my truck, and I dug up the sod and flipped it over so no one else could read it."

He didn't just grimace, he clenched his teeth, grimaced, shut his eyes, sighed, stomped his foot, and in general looked as if he were sick to his stomach. "You didn't?! Tell me you didn't!"

I backed away from him, alarmed that he might take his job a bit too seriously. "I'm really sorry. But yeah, the sod is all cut up and flipped over. I reckon I was just mad."

Molly moved between us and said, "Sir, perhaps Chris wasn't thinking logically…or forensically."

His grimace eased into discomfort, which drifted slowly into resignation. Finally he shrugged his shoulders and clasped his hands together. He moved around Molly, extended both index fingers like the barrel of a gun, and pointed them at me. "Ya know, Chris, you really stink as a crime scene investigator."

"Yessir. I should probably stick to golf."

Molly spoke from behind him. "I'll encourage him, sir, to stick to golf."

But I could not keep myself from staying involved; I was determined to help. Before I left, I asked Jonathan for a photo of the matching B. He had several four-by-six copies laying on his table, and after a moment of hesitation, he agreed to give me one. "Just don't tamper with anything else that might be used for evidence."

I felt bad for messing up his work. But what I didn't tell him was that I had my own idea of how to identify the criminal. I thanked him for the photo and motioned for Molly to follow me out.

Jonathan cleared his throat and said, "Oh, I need you to sign for that photo." Then he pointed to a form on his desk.

I went to the desk and grabbed a pen and said, "Sure, no problem."

Then he said, "Sign your *full* name, please."

"Okay." So I signed in my best cursive: Christopher Bryce Hackett.

He came over and picked up the form and stared at my middle name for a couple seconds.

"Interesting signature, Chris," he said. Then he broke into a grin and said, "Only kidding! Just jabbing you a bit after messing up that sod. I assure you that you're not on the suspect list."

All we needed, a prankster investigator. "Can we go now?" I asked.

He set the form back on his desk. "Yes…you two enjoy your weekend." From the look on his face, he regretted his little tease. But I wrote that off as bad timing, aware that I'd done the same on many occasions.

Unmoved by the exchange, Molly tapped Jonathan on the shoulder and said, "Sir, could you share with us the names of any *legitimate* suspects?"

He frowned and in general acted as if he would refuse. But finally he relented and told us that he planned on investigating a few people and would share the names only if we gave him our oath not to get involved. When pressed further, he leaned over his desk and scrawled some words on a sheet of paper. He handed the piece of paper to Molly, and the two of us stopped in his doorway and read the suspects' names:

A) Various and covert political operatives
B) Mr. Roycroft
C) Lin Givens

Still in the doorway, I explained to Jonathan that choice A— various and covert political operatives—were the only true suspects. Mr Roycroft was simply too nice of a guy, and Lin Givens was so obsessed with Adam's shortcomings that she'd never find time to commit arson.

Jonathan acted as if he accepted my explanations and told us again to enjoy our weekend. Everything still moved too slowly, however, and as we walked outside the building and onto the sidewalk I told Molly of my personal investigative method.

"We need the name of a former president whose last name began with 'B'," I said and noted her confused reaction. "And we also need his place in the numerical order, if he was the eighteenth or twenty-third or whatever."

She stopped next to my truck and counted on her fingertips, three trips through her left hand. "The fifteenth president was Buchanan."

I opened the door for her and said, "You have *all* the presidents memorized?"

"It's a job requirement," she said and climbed in.

Before pulling onto the highway, I explained to her my method might take a while, yet I figured that was what I had the most of—time.

No one has more time on their hands than an unmarried, unemployed golf instructor.

Inside the lobby of Charleston Democratic headquarters, we feigned interest in everything liberal and blended with dozens of volunteers. Gathered in twos and threes, they assembled signs, unpacked boxes of flyers, and chatted about the upcoming elections.

Molly and I blended well. Awesomely, in fact. This was due partly to our visit to a CVS to purchase hair gel—the slick-backed look for me—and two pairs of nonmatching, nonprescription wire-rimmed glasses. These, along with the free patriotic donkey caps and nametags we were given outside the front door of headquarters, disguised us about as well as my small budget allowed. I was now Christopher *Hammett*, Democratic volunteer, and Molly was now Milly Conner, also a volunteer.

Smiling warmly, we moved between clusters of anti-this and anti-that until someone patted me on the back and said, "We're gonna stick it to the Republicans in November, aren't we?!"

"Yessir," I replied, not missing a beat. "No doubt about it. No more wars for oil."

He grinned big, picked up an armful of campaign signs, and toted them out to his car.

I had no such things in my arms. The only thing I toted was a stack of sixty copies of a questionnaire I'd brought with me, which was quite brief as far as questionnaires go. It consisted of a single question, plus the promise that all who got the question right (no asking fellow volunteers for the answer!) would be entered into a drawing for a free set of Nike golf clubs.

The question was typed in big letters:

*Can you name the fifteenth President of the
United States? Please write his name in cursive:*

Beneath the answer line was a space for the questionee to write their name and phone number. My idea may have seemed far-fetched, but it was all I had, and Molly agreed that it at least held possibilities. It was time to compare the penmanship of liberals with the penmanship of conservatives. And a free give-away never hurt, either.

A coordinator for the volunteers toiled behind a bumper-stickered desk, her phone at one ear, her hands stuffing cards into envelopes. I waited patiently until she caught my gaze and put one hand over her phone. "Yes?" she inquired. "May I help you?"

"Um, we're helping out west of the Ashley River and wanted to ask if you could distribute these to all the volunteers. It's something to thank them…just a short questionnaire with a chance to win a set of golf clubs."

Molly leaned in and said, "They're really great clubs. We'll return to pick a winner in a couple of days."

Apparently in a great hurry, the lady pointed at her desk and said, "Leave the questionnaires there. I'll get to it as soon as I can. Thanks."

A brief wave and she was back on the phone, talking excitedly about the momentum of the campaigns.

On the way out we grabbed a handful of flyers, just to appear genuine.

Twenty minutes later we donned elephant caps, entered Republican headquarters, and held in our hands another sixty copies of my questionnaire. I was now Christopher Hammond, and Molly was now Mildred Cusackski.

We stuck our nametags to our shirts, and it was then that I had to question Molly's name choice. "Mildred? *Cusackski?*"

She pressed her nametag firmly into place. "Mildred is a nice conservative name, Christopher. Though I admit Cusackski may stretch credibility."

We mingled, shook hands with strangers, mingled some more. The Republicans dressed more conservatively than their opponents, and yet their energy level and confidence ran just as high. In fact, on the back wall they showed on a video screen a herd of rampaging elephants traversing a jungle. Molly called this a somewhat shortsighted video, since the herd had obviously eaten enormous quantities of food earlier in the day and were now leaving enormous messes for whoever came behind them on the path.

"Not the most awe-inspiring political rah-rah," Molly said, shaking her head as if she could do better, much better.

Dozens of volunteers then burst into chants of predicted victory—"Elephant romp, elephant romp!"—and this over-whelmed the video, plus the blaring voice of a local radio talk show host.

Molly squeezed between groups of volunteers and handed her stack of questionnaires to a coordinator, a clean-cut man who, although he looked too young for the job, wore a nametag that read "Coordinator."

"What is this?" he asked.

I pointed to the large lettering and interrupted. "Just something to reward the hardworking volunteers, sir. An easy little trivia question that will qualify them for a drawing for a new set of golf clubs."

He smiled and said, "Republicans do love to golf. . . ."

"Can you hand them out?" Molly asked with a humble smile. "We'll pick them up in a few days."

He glanced around the room at the chanting volunteers. "I'll be glad to."

Molly and I pushed open the twin exit doors and left the Republicans, convinced that somewhere in the city of Charleston lived a political operative whose handwriting boasted a long tail on the letter B. We were determined to help find this person. And when we did, well, I hoped I would have enough sense to let the authorities take over.

In my truck we tore off our nametags and deemed our plan a good beginning. We'd wait a day or two, collect the questionnaires, then compare the handwritings of lefties and righties.

I stuck my key in the ignition but did not crank the engine. "Would you like to go on a date now?" I asked.

Molly snapped her seat belt shut and said, "Sure. But was this questionnaire thing the only idea you had for today?"

"For now, yes. You have something different?"

Molly slowly bit her lip, shook her head. "Let me think on it." For a moment she rubbed her temple, but then shrugged as if to signal the topic was over for now. "So, what kind of date do you have in mind?"

"Well, Miss Cusackski, the first romantic thirty minutes will be spent at Lowe's, getting some equipment prices for Allstate."

"Oh boy."

"The second thirty minutes will be spent scoping a piece of barren land."

"Whoo. I'll be sure to wear my little black dress."

I smiled and cranked the engine. "Then we'll have the entire rest of the day to tour historic downtown Charleston."

"Now you're talkin', Golf Man."

22

LESSON FOR TODAY

**On or off the course, a shared stroll is
a great time for discovery.**

In the historic section of Charleston, pedigree is often as valued as real estate. Beside their whitewashed antebellum homes, fourth-generation owners poke around their lawns beneath overgrown magnolias, avoiding eye contact with tourists and, in general, displaying the privileged air of entitlement. If you happen to meet one, the owner might repeat your last name as if tasting it for a familiar spice. "Cusack? No, sorry, don't know that name. You must be from up north."

This was Molly's experience as we walked the shaded sidewalks south of Broad Street. She'd tried to introduce herself to an elderly lady outside a lush-gardened, pastel blue house and received that very response. Molly laughed off the experience and, a block later, referred to the owner as a "grits and caviar Republican."

We crossed the street and headed for the waterfront, where the homes were colossal, the views outstanding. "Just curious, Mol—how would you classify *me*?"

"Hmmm," she said, on her toes now and peering out at Fort Sumter. "A grits and golf Republican?"

"I'd accept that."

With craned necks we admired another row of Old South habitations, and it was here, while distracted by the charm and vintage of our surroundings, that our fingers interlocked and we held hands. We walked out to the tip of downtown and sat on a bench beneath an oak, a tree that looked as old as the homes it fronted.

"This is not going to be easy, Chris," she said and rolled her foot around the top of some acorns.

"You mean figuring out the long tail on the letter B?"

"No, I mean long-distance dating."

Before I replied I paused to consider the possibilities. Although I was free to rebuild anywhere and wanted to be near Molly, I had no real interest in establishing a Hack's of Washington DC. Then again, I could see where employing Cack and his bullhorn in such environs—around all those politicians and pundits—might offer unending comedy and no shortage of revenue. But no, that was off my radar. Mainly because I loved Charleston's climate, plus its proximity to great seafood.

What I determined to tell Molly mentioned nothing of climates or DC; I grasped the real gist of what she was asking. "Molly, this may sound a tad premature, or maybe it won't, but know this—if we determine we want each other in a permanent way, we will make it happen. Whatever it takes."

My comment seemed to press Molly against the back of the bench. She sat staring straight ahead, eyes glancing left and right, mouth agape. What I had said to her had come from the heart, but it had also grown out of a conversation I'd had with Pauly Three Seeds. On his fourth date with his future wife, he'd employed a similar approach and said it worked wonders for her confidence level. His insight on the matter led him to conclude that the average single woman is so used to hearing vagueness from men instead of initiative, that such a reply would, in most cases, render the woman temporarily speechless.

Pauly Three Seeds was right. For one minute, perhaps a minute and a half, Molly said nothing. I hoped I hadn't scared her off, that she would not suddenly jump from the bench and announce she had to catch an early flight home. Instead she turned to me and said, "Ya know, Chris, I wish politicians were that forthcoming."

I stood in front of the bench, faced the flag flying over the fort, and performed a politician's exaggerated salute. "Vote for Golf Man, Senator of Duffers."

She reached out and tugged me back to the bench. "For you, Golf Man, I might just rig the voting machines."

The way we eased in and out of serious and lighthearted topics had been evident to me from the first date. I figured we would sit there a while and enjoy this growing sense of compatibility, but the light of day faded fast into an October chill, and when she rubbed her arms and shivered I knew it was time to make dinner plans.

Yet another reason I was attracted to this woman—she gave great signals.

At a corner table in The Boathouse, our meal unfolded beneath soft lights and even softer music, the high point a tie between the sharing of our entrees and the story Molly told about growing up in Virginia. The short version was the week she turned eleven, she and her best friend, Hannah, also eleven, decided to visit a new Kmart just down the street from their neighborhood. It was July, and since curfew was dark-thirty, they wandered into the Kmart at 8:30 p.m., just to look around and buy some candy. They ended up in the clothing section and, after weighing the consequences and deciding this was worth it, hid inside a rack of sport coats. The store closed. Lights dimmed. Parents panicked. They were discovered at 1:00 a.m., asleep in plastic canoes and wearing men's work boots, pink prom-like dresses, and fake coonskin caps.

"And the consequences?" I asked, racking my memory for a similar story.

"Grounded for a month, plus we had to pick up litter in the parking lot before the store reopened."

I had no similar story, nothing to compete, anyway. Much of the hilarity of my life had taken place at my driving range. I supposed some people don't find their real sense of humor until they find their niche, and this had been the case for me.

The restaurant's back deck overlooked the Intracoastal Waterway, and we made our way out there after dinner. Moonlight by itself would have been enough, but tonight we had moonlight, starlight, slow-moving waters, and the chill of autumn—a great spot for a first kiss.

Brief but enjoyable, she called it. "And perfectly timed," she added a few seconds later. At the railing we watched a pair of sailboats lower their sails and drift by in the waterway.

Molly nudged her foot against mine and said, "Chris, tomorrow I think we should—"

"Should what?" I wondered what kind of lovey-dovey thoughts had invaded her mind.

She peered out at the moonlight's watery shimmer. "Tomorrow I think we should check with the Democrats at noon, the Republicans around two or three, and collect any and all completed questionnaires."

Ah, yes...romance.

23

LESSON FOR TODAY

The game, like a new relationship,
does not so much *mold* character as it
does *expose* character (and on occasion,
intelligence).

Already penmanship excited us. Even before the receptionist at
Democratic headquarters handed Molly the stack of completed
questionnaires—and a six-inch stack of pamphlets to distribute at our leisure—I anticipated the analysis of many variations
of the letter B. What I did not, or could not, anticipate was the
diversity of opinion on who held the status of fifteenth president
of the United States.

Stack in hand, we rushed through hordes of Saturday volunteers and hurried to my truck. Ten minutes later I was Christopher Hammond again, and Molly, Mildred C., exchanging
smiles and pleasantries with overconfident Republicans.

The smiling man seated at the information desk said, "So you're
the two offering the golf club giveaway. What kind of clubs?"

"A set of Nike irons," I gushed. "They're brand new." I had
stored the clubs in my closet, having acquired them from a
sales rep during a summer demo day at my range.

"Well then," he said, motioning to the entries, "I just might win because I've had all the presidents memorized since fifth grade."

Molly congratulated him on his knowledge, and I considered offering him a gold star, but I kept my mouth shut and accepted the return of my one-question questionnaires. Then we rushed out to my truck, drove to a neighborhood bagel shop, found a corner booth, and went about the task of discovering the guilty party.

We began with the Democratic stack of questionnaires and read through them quickly. Molly peeled them from the stack one by one, muttering, "wow," "shocking," and "imbecile," as we studied each page.

James Buchanan
Calvin James Coolidge
Jefferson Buchanan
Ulysses F. Grant
James E. Buchanan
F. Scott Fitzgerald
William Jefferson Buchanan
James Buchanan
Thomas Filmore Buchanan
Hillary Rodham Rushmore
James G. Buchanan
Dishonest Abe
James "No WMDs" Buchanan
Herbert Ike Buchanan
Buchanan Jefferson Hoover
Teddy Roosevelt
James "Antiwar" Buchanan

From the stack we found four entries whose handwriting employed long tails on the letter B. Three of them were from males, one from a female. I set these four aside, and Molly began sifting through the Republican stack.

"Not much better," she said and passed these one at a time into my waiting hands.

James G. Buchanan
Abraham Lincoln
James K. Buchanan
Stonewall Jackson
Boris Yeltsin
James "Rush" Buchanan
Richard Millhouse Buchanan
James "I Luv Red States" Buchanan
Abe
Not Dubya
J. Pro-life Buchanan
William Henry Harrison
James Buchanan
James Taylor
Jesse James

Republican handwriting also displayed, in three instances, a long tail on the B. Two from men, one from a woman.

Mass confusion set in. Four Democrats, three Republicans—this was not supposed to be a close race. Exit polls had shown the battleground signatures of the Democrats winning in a landslide. But now the total suspects numbered seven.

Molly studied each one, arranged them in order of gender. I rearranged them in order of suspicion. Then I rearranged them again according to size of signature. Then I remembered the arson investigator felt sure the spray painter was male, so I set aside the two female suspects and flipped twice more through the males.

"You feel positive it's a man?" Molly asked.

"Yep. I do."

Our next move seemed obvious: I would call each one, thank them for their hard work on the campaign, and casually ask what they were doing on the night of September 23.

But first I called the arson investigator and asked for another update.

At the sound of my voice, Jonathan sighed. "Chris, this may sound out of left field, but it might be good to get away from this altogether for a few days. Why don't you concentrate on rebuilding your business, use that effort to keep yourself occupied."

I didn't tell him that I was already occupied with deciphering the penmanship of lefties and righties. All I did was thank him and promise not to bother him again until he called with his next update.

Before I could hang up, however, he said, "Chris, I need you to answer something for me."

"Um... sure."

"You and Molly aren't trying to solve this case yourselves, are you?"

A pause, a cough, a longer pause. "What makes you think that?"

"My secretary said someone called in yesterday asking if there were any books she could recommend on deciphering male handwriting. That wouldn't be a phone call that you—"

My first instinct was to tell a little white golfer lie. But my second instinct was a reminder that this man was on my side. "Okay, sir, Molly and I had this idea. But you should know that we've whittled the suspects down to just five men. Three Democrats and two Republicans. All of them local campaign volunteers. I got their signatures, and each one puts a long tail on the letter B."

From my cell phone I heard laughter. Then a snort and more laughter. "You really should get away from this, Chris. Get a part-time job, anything at all."

"Why? You don't want us to check the alibis of these suspects?"

"It's highly unlikely that the arsonist would be working the very next week as a local campaign volunteer. Even if a political party is connected to this, the perpetrator would likely be an operative, someone paid off with a bag of money and told to disguise his work so it would look like either party could have done it."

Embarrassed by my feeble efforts, I said good-bye to Jonathan, shut my phone, and spun it on the table in mock frustration. "He says I should stick to rebuilding the business."

Molly thought hard on this suggestion. "Maybe God is shouting at you not to get involved in crime solving."

I gulped a pint of pride and tore my questionnaires in half. Molly shrugged and said she was glad she no longer had to think up names like Cusackski.

She then plucked my cell phone from the table and opened it. She pressed a couple buttons and said, "Hmmm, looks like you've made four calls to the investigator this week, but only two calls to me. Bad ratio, Golf Man. Tsk Tsk."

Her ability to amuse me was unequaled. I told her this and reached for her hand and helped her from the booth.

"Since we're already in jeans, wanna go scope another piece of land?"

"As long as there's no snakes."

Molly was not only helpful, but understanding. We left my truck parked along a frontage road next to Highway 17 in Mt. Pleasant, and for long minutes we stood scanning the parcel, shielding our eyes from the glare and admiring rich soil that looked like it would host well the grass seed I could sprinkle into it.

I pointed to the east end and then to the west. "How's it look to you, Mol?"

She wasn't the type to just agree with anything a man said, and she did not fudge her answer. "Looks like barren ground to me, except for those ugly bushes on the far side. How does it look like to *you*? You're the range expert."

"Looks flat enough, and possibly long enough."

She moved closer, picked up a stick, and swung it in slow motion. "And just where would I get my private golf lessons?"

With the heel of my shoe I carved a large M in the dirt. "Right here?"

She inspected the spot and then used her own heel to carve a big NPA a few feet to the side.

"What is that for?"

"This is where your sign goes that reads 'No Politics Allowed.'"

I shook my head at the memory. "Lesson learned."

For twenty minutes we walked the width and breadth of the land, Molly gushing that this was great exercise, never mind the occasional ant mound.

I noted that the afternoon sun shone from behind the future hitting area, a big plus. Always one to double-check details, I tromped the breadth one more time, trying to fit a golf shop, thirty-six hitting mats, a practice putting green, and a maintenance shed onto the property.

I wondered if Molly had already grown bored, but as I walked back in her direction over all that red dirt, she waved and shouted, "I know what you're thinking, Chris! I can see your mind turning from here."

I smiled and held my tongue until I was within a few yards of her. "Okay, what am I thinking? Tell me."

She made a kind of beginner's golf swing. "You're picturing slicers slicing, hackers hacking, and duffers duffing. Right?" She looked almost as giddy as she did confident. "Am I right?"

The woman rendered me defenseless. "How in the world did you guess that?"

"I was just trying to put myself in a golf teacher's shoes." She motioned to the real estate sign posted just this side of the frontage road. "Want me to call the number and ask how much?"

The sign was huge and read FOR LEASE. I stared at it for a moment, trying to guesstimate both a leasing price and a sales price. "Thanks," I said, "but I should probably make the call myself."

I noted the phone number on the sign, pressed the appropriate digits on my cell, and in seconds found myself speaking to the manager of the leasing company.

"Oh, that's *prime* property," she said after I told her where I was standing.

"Somehow I expected you to say that."

Next she recited her credentials: member of board of Real-tors, graduate of an appraisal institute, top sales person for eight straight years. I figured she was just bragging a bit, but perhaps her motives lay in the realm of softening the blow. They wanted $5,500 per month for leasing the land, with two months' deposit up front, plus they retained a sixty-day notice should some developer want to buy the land outright. In comparison, Mr. Vignatti had leased his land to me for $1,950 per month, a deal that I didn't fully appreciate until this moment.

With great trepidation I asked the buyout price of the property. With no trepidation at all, the Realtor said, "Two point four million, sir."

I thanked her and ended the call. For a minute I just kicked the red dirt, as if to punish it for being so costly. Then I turned and noted the sheer size of the sign. It stood more than ten feet tall and at least that wide; this alone should have been warning enough. The land had looked so right, though. Three hundred forty yards deep by four hundred ten yards wide.

In a fleeting fit of frustration I picked up a rock—about the size of a golf ball, which seemed appropriate—and hurled it at the unpainted back of the sign. It bounced off a post, however, and ricocheted back into my right big toe, protected only by the old sneaker I'd worn to walk the land. Even with my shoe on, the impact stung.

Molly suppressed a laugh as I hopped on my left leg, and it was then that her cell rang. Her glance at the caller ID told me this was probably business. Her frown confirmed just that.

Interesting how one can tell the nature of a call from mere observation: The person you're with turns partially away, head tilted down, her free hand cupping the phone, lots of nods accompanying each recitation of "Yes, boss, I understand."

Twice Molly looked over and frowned with sympathy—she even stomped her foot on the ground before she ended the call.

I leaned against the side of my truck, waiting for her to speak. She walked straight up to me, stuffed her phone in her pocket, and clasped both of my hands in hers. "Chris, they want me on a plane to Richmond in two hours. I have to cover a debate."

Though disappointed at the news, I was moved by the gesture. She could have just said it; she didn't have to come over and say it with such feeling.

I probably should have shown some affection and hugged her, but instead I embraced maledom and employed logic. "But I thought they gave you *three* days?"

She squeezed my hands. "It's election year. Sorry, I have to do what they ask."

I still wasn't ready to give up. "But—but I was gonna take you out in my johnboat and show you the pelicans."

"I'm really sorry, Chris." With her head she motioned to the highway. "Want to follow me to the airport, say good-bye there?"

First I drove her to her hotel and waited in the lobby while she grabbed her suitcase and checked out. In the parking lot I agreed to follow her and meet up at the United ticket counter. She tossed her luggage into her rental car, and we sped for the airport.

I parked on the first floor of a parking deck and walked toward the terminal, where the sound of jets ascending and descending made me yearn to take a trip myself. Possibly to DC. And possibly in the near future.

Inside the terminal, Molly bought her ticket and joined me beside some fake potted plants, directly across from the escalators. I handed her a golf ball on which I had written in red Sharpie *Vote for Golf Man.*

She smiled and tucked it into her purse. "I had a blast," she said.

"I'll see you soon."

Our parting hug lasted longer than our parting kiss, though both were enjoyable. Then she pulled her luggage onto the escalator and rode it backward, facing me.

I waved.

Ten feet above me and rising, she waved back. Then she said, "I keep thinking about that sod you dug up."

"No hidden clues there," I replied with upturned face. "Just a few yards of sod with gas poured on it."

Now twenty feet above me, she looked down over the metal steps and said, "Hmmm. Interesting."

24

LESSON FOR TODAY

In golf (and dating), being aggressive
at the wrong time can lead to disaster.
But woe unto competition if one is
aggressive at the *proper* time.

My mailbox lying in the gutter offered the first clue that something was wrong in suburbia. I had just returned home from the airport, and had ended a cell call to Cack about where we should relocate the business.

In a generally good mood—I knew I'd see Molly again soon and felt confident that Cack and I could find the right piece of land—I eased into the first few feet of driveway and craned my neck to look down at the fallen mailbox. Probably just kids whopping boxes with a baseball bat. A minor inconvenience, at most. Nothing to ruin my day.

Then I looked across my yard at my house and saw familiar words, huge and blue: **"Biased Loser"** spray painted on the vinyl siding to the left of my front door. I stopped and backed up my truck for a wider view, scanning windows to see if someone was inside. Nothing moved.

My heart raced. My breath quickened. *To call authorities or not to call. What if he's still here?* Urgency pressed upon me, and

I searched the floorboard of my truck for any kind of weapon. In the backseat lay the only weaponry I possessed—my golf clubs.

I chose the 4-iron.

Out of the truck, I stepped softly through my front yard. Strange, sneaking up on your own home. Some forty feet from the front steps, I cringed when the muffled ring of my cell phone sounded from deep in my pants pocket.

I ducked behind a holly bush and pulled the phone out.

"Chris, where are you?" the voice asked. It was Jonathan, the arson investigator.

I kept my voice low. "I just arrived at my house. Looks like whoever set fire to my range just paid a visit to my neighborhood."

"Are you *in* your house?!" he demanded, his tone frantic.

"No, I just got here. I'm behind a bush in the front yard."

"Did you just leave the airport?"

"About an hour ago, yes…but how'd you know that?"

"Your girlfriend called me from the terminal. She had an idea, and it led me to one of your competitors."

"But how did she—"

"Stay put. Better yet, lock yourself in your truck. Police are on the way."

Sirens sounded from down my street. I retreated to my truck and saw blue lights flashing from a block away—two patrol cars, closing fast. I spun around to look again at my house and saw a tall guy in jeans run out the side door. He sprinted across my deck toward the backyard fence, dropping a spray can as he fled.

He'll get away. And that cannot happen.

I ran up my driveway, toting my 4-iron like a war club. I had no idea if I'd hurl the club at the guy or just threaten him with it. On the other hand, I had no idea if he had a knife, or a gun, or nothing at all. Sirens grew loud behind me. Cops in my driveway. I passed the right side of my house and ran onto a lawn that had never, to my knowledge, hosted a foot chase. Tires skidded just behind me, and before I knew it—I was not even across my backyard yet—a strong hand tugged my shirt collar.

"Stay in your truck, Mr. Hackett!" the cop shouted and pulled me backward.

I fell to the ground but jumped back to my feet.

Two officers ran after the guy, who weaved between trees and scaled my fence and turned left behind the neighbor's home. An officer in the second car bolted past me and repeated the instruction for me to stay in my truck.

I loped back down the driveway to my truck and almost obeyed. Instead of waiting *inside* my truck, I stood beside the driver's door, heart pounding with adrenaline, hoping to see the officers drag the guy out of the woods and through my yard and into one of their squad cars. But those woods were thick, and the guy in jeans had a huge head start.

Time seemed suspended. A cop chase on my property felt surreal, nothing like watching a cop chase on TV. Plus I felt violated, even a bit vindictive.

For long minutes I heard nothing, only the inner noise of a speculating, hyperactive mind. *Have they subdued him? Has he subdued them?*

Then I heard yelling, first behind my house and then behind the neighbor's. Then, two houses north of mine, the suspect sprinted between hedges, across my neighbor's front yard, and back down toward the street.

The officers chased after him but this guy was fast. He kept running, extending his lead, and every synapse in my body screamed to join the chase, to seek my own justice.

And I did.

Sort of.

As the suspect ran into the street with long, loping strides, I reached into the backseat to my golf bag, grabbed a handful of golf balls, and quickly dropped them to the ground. The suspect sprinted at an angle for the opposite woods. He never saw me take aim.

Four-iron in hand, I led him by several feet, aiming low, since I didn't want to hit him in the head. *Just like at the range,* I told myself.

Thwack. Wide left.

Thwack. Wide right.

Thwack. Wide right again.

Thwack…The fourth ball took off in a low, skim-the-grass trajectory, rose as backspin joined forward momentum, and slammed into the guy's rib cage. Or perhaps just below the rib cage—regardless, he fell sprawling into the gutter some hundred yards away, elbows and knees sliding on pavement. The ball had knocked the breath out of him.

Stunned by what I'd just done, I studied the head of my club as if it held magical powers. *Not a bad shot considering I had no time to stretch or warm up.*

The three officers ran into the street and pounced on the guy. Handcuffs snapped shut. More yelling. On his feet and writhing, the guy cursed the officers for shooting him in the ribs.

The cop who'd handcuffed him shoved the guy toward a squad car and said, "No one shot you, sir."

The guy shouted, "You shot me in the *rib cage,* man!"

Since there was no blood on his shirt—just road rash on his elbows—I wondered if the guy had lost his mind or if he really believed he'd been shot.

The officers loaded him into the second squad car, and that car sped away. That's when I noticed neighbors old and young gathering in their front yards and peering down the street at us.

I waved meekly. None of them waved back.

Then the two officers who had pulled me from the chase came striding my way, stern looks on their faces. I backed against my truck, wondering if they might arrest me too. I just stood there as if I'd been deputized, my 4-iron held proudly at my side, a sentry with his rifle.

The two officers stopped a couple feet from me, both with hands on hips, both shaking their heads.

The shorter one said, "Mr. Hackett, I can't believe you just did that. We told you to stay inside your truck."

Then the two of them burst into grins. The taller one said, "That's the wildest golf shot I ever seen. How'd you do that?"

I gave them my best aw shucks expression and said, "Just regular practice, sir."

In a kind of curious silence they stared at my club as if it were some new form of thug-stopping weaponry.

Aware that I had their full attention, I gripped my 4-iron and made a slow, instructive type of swing, offering to these gentlemen of law enforcement a kind of postchase miniclinic. They looked keenly interested in my technique, so I handed the club to the taller one and watched as he pressed his holster back and assumed a golf stance there in my yard.

I reached out to adjust his grip. "Remember, Officer, you are the machine gun; the golf balls are your bullets."

25

LESSON FOR TODAY

**Sometimes people cheat—and many
times they get caught.**

The guy who set fire to my golf shop was neither Democrat nor
Republican. Oddly, he had no voting record at all, no connec-
tion to a political party. Randolph Matthew Newbury owned a
competing golf range on the north side of Charleston.

From my back deck I relayed this news to Molly via cell
phone. It was shortly before midnight, and I'd just finished
removing the graffiti from my house. She'd just finished covering the debate and was sitting on the steps of an auditorium in
Richmond.

"It's true, Molly, I helped subdue the guy."

She laughed. "You're telling me that you, Golf Man, nabbed
the suspect ahead of the cops? What'd you do, wrestle the guy
into submission all by yourself?"

"Nope, just used the tools of my profession." Though that
event had lent a small sense of satisfaction, it was Molly's role
that intrigued me. "What Golf Man wants to know is, how did
you figure out *who* to suspect?"

"Just before I boarded the plane in Charleston, I stopped

thinking about the shape of the letter B and started thinking instead about the repeated use of the word 'Bias.' The arsonist had already used the phrase on your sidewalk with the spray paint."

"So you're saying it was *repetition*? Just those few words burned into the sod?"

"Well, the second usage on your grass meant that he was really overemphasizing the word 'bias.' And I knew from my dealings with the political world that anytime a candidate overemphasizes an issue and begins name-calling, it means he's trying to distract attention from something else."

"Which was?"

"The fact that the suspect was just trying to use election-year hysterics as cover while he destroyed some competition."

This took me a moment to process. The same woman who makes the suggestion that fosters the destruction of my business also figures out who did it—from three hundred miles away? "Why didn't I think of that?"

Her laugh retreated into a stifled snort. "Probably because the whole political angle at your range was new to you. I've been around such shysters my entire career." She stopped talking then, and I heard muffled voices in the line, as if she were saying good night to people at the auditorium. "Sorry, Chris, I had to speak with a candidate's chatty wife. But I'm back now and need to be up front with you about something."

"Shoot."

"I sorta met that Newbury guy once…the arsonist. Of course, I didn't know he was capable of such a crime when I met him. And I'd forgotten all about him until I got to the airport and started dwelling on that sod."

I mouthed a silent "what?" into my phone. She would have to explain this. "You *met* him? How could—"

"For maybe thirty seconds, Chris. But yeah, I met him. About a week before I wandered onto your range, I checked out his for the same idea I suggested to you. But I thought his place was too small. Then, when I visited your place and saw what you and Cack had going, well, that was it."

"Love at first sight?"

"Well, political insult at first sight."

For a moment I struggled to grasp that Molly had met Newbury. But the more I thought about it, the more I figured if my local grocery store had burned down, I wouldn't automatically suspect another grocer across town had committed the crime. The whole idea of "eliminate your competition via violence" had never registered with me.

We talked of our recent date and told each other how much we'd enjoyed it. This led quickly to a discussion of when we could see each other again. Her schedule was packed till after the elections; mine was about to be overwhelmed by the rebuilding of the business. We agreed that this was going to be hard. Not impossible, just hard.

Before we hung up, however, I told her how much I appreciated her support and powers of deduction and that this was one time when Adam really did appreciate Eve for her mind.

She replied in much the same manner I expected. "Sure, sure. That's what all you Adams say."

Apparently Newbury had developed a possessive crush on Molly, saw her on the news promoting my range instead of his, and deduced (correctly) that the two of us were dating. Jonathan explained this via a morning phone call, describing the motivation as a double dose of jealousy.

"Not one but two scoops of envy, Chris," Jonathan said.

"Money and... that woman. Each on its own is enough to make a man crazy."

Combined, I supposed they could send a man into a fit, but into a fire-setting monster? I shared this thought with Jonathan, and he shared more details of how he identified Newbury. "First we went to his range, checked the soles of a discarded pair of sneakers, and found green and white pea gravel stuck in the treads. He wasn't at his range, though. He had headed for your house."

Newbury had a record too—auto theft, breaking and entering, plus two trips to a mental rehabilitation facility.

What stunned me was the guy's propensity for violence. Not the retaliatory violence that I heard about so often in the news, but the premeditated variety. Not only was he jealous of the attention and monies Hack's had pulled in during the political cycle, and not only was he envious of my relationship with Molly, he'd figured it would be easy to torch a competing range and make it look like a political operative did it. According to Jonathan, Mr. Newbury's range was averaging just over eighty dollars a day in revenue during the same time Hack's averaged over three hundred per day.

Newbury also threatened to sue me for hitting him in the gut with a golf ball. But when the authorities found in his jeans pocket my silver Movado watch that'd he lifted from my office the night of the fire—my initials were etched on the back side of the watch—he reconsidered his threat.

I told Jonathan he'd certainly earned his salary and even offered him free golf lessons after I rebuilt my business. But he didn't play the game. Said he preferred deep-sea fishing with some buddies from Georgetown.

He explained that the arson committed at Hack's was one of the easier cases he'd ever investigated. On the day that Newbury had chosen to spray paint my house, Jonathan was checking the last month's sales for one particular item at every hardware store in the Charleston metro area.

The one item, of course, was plastic gas containers. He'd found that on September 22, the afternoon before the torching, a Wal-Mart in North Charleston had sold five gas containers at 4:31 p.m., five more at 4:38 p.m., and four more at 4:46 p.m. Fourteen five-gallon containers in fifteen minutes, plus a can of blue spray paint. All paid for with the same debit card at registers two, nine, and sixteen. Then, after Molly had called him from the airport, Jonathan checked with Wal-Mart again and found that the same person had returned that morning and purchased two more cans of blue spray paint. At my house, Newbury just wanted to rub it in, we supposed. But as with a golfer who swings too hard too many times, hazards often await. It proved horrible timing as well. Newbury's triple bogey.

Cack, ever conscious of promotional opportunity, informed our local media of the 4-iron incident. During the following days the publicity garnered from halting a suspect with a golf shot turned out to be greater than the publicity garnered for allowing political parties to whack balls at each other. A local news team even requested permission to come out to my house and have me recreate the shot for their cameras. I thought this a bit much—overkill actually. So I refused.

Besides, I had a business to rebuild. And the only news correspondent I wanted to talk with lived in DC.

26

LESSON FOR TODAY

In Southern states, occasional
encounters with wildlife are an
accepted part of any outdoor activity.

"Three hundred and twenty-two yards, boss man," Cack said
into his new walkie-talkie.

With proceeds from the insurance settlement we'd purchased the powerful kind, two of them, with a range of more
than one mile. Today Cack employed his as he stood on the
far end of a rectangular piece of land not far from the Ashley
River, separated from me by the distance he'd called out and
also by twenty-two acres of weeds.

"Ten-four," I said into my mouthpiece and walked another
twenty paces to the west, along the frontage road. "Now what's
the distance from here?"

He paralleled my movement and stopped again. "Three-
nineteen," he said.

We met halfway across the parcel and compared notes. Cack
then handed me my measuring instrument, a device called
a range finder, which utilizes GPS to calculate distances to
within an accuracy of six inches. Just for fun I pointed the

range finder in the direction of our nation's capital, silently renamed it a "Molly finder," and waited for it to give me a distance. The tiny screen read, *Data Not Available.*

"Just what are you measuring now?" Cack asked and tucked his pencil behind his ear. "You were pointing that thing at DC, weren't ya?"

"Let's get back to work, pardner."

I wanted to double-check our figures, especially since at the back of the property, just past the boundary stakes, appeared to be a wetlands area. Cack hurried off in that direction while I remained at the frontage road, range finder in hand.

As an amateur survey team, the two of us concluded within the hour that this land was nearly level and that it also had the necessary depth and width to accommodate a new Hack's Golf Learning Center. The thrust of the new business, however, was an issue I'd already debated, considered, and resolved. In fact, my plan was to call Molly tonight and tell her about my new idea: to make the new Hack's more kid-centric and less adult-centric.

Whether the children of Charleston dreamt little "I-just-wanna-hit-the-ball" golf dreams or big "I-wanna-be-great" golf dreams, I wanted to offer them the hope, the fun, and the instruction to help them reach their goals.

When I was a kid, my dream was to play the PGA Tour. The dream first ripened at age ten, just after I'd defeated J. T. Turner for the 10–11-year-old bracket of the city junior championship. Friends since first grade, he and I had walked up the eighteenth fairway that day boasting of where we'd be in twelve years—traveling the country, heck, even the globe, and competing against the world's best.

J. T. said he'd live in a big house in Florida and drive a Porsche. I told him I'd live in a big house in Arizona and drive a Ferrari. J. T.'s dream lasted until junior year of high school, when he confessed to me that he couldn't even beat the kids at our school, much less compete on a national level. Said he was going to play it smart, get a college degree, and enter corporate America, perhaps get married and start a family. And he did exactly that.

My own dream stayed alive through high school and beyond—I won several tournaments and had scholarship offers to play at the collegiate level. I chose Georgia, where my dream grew into an all-consuming, determined obsession.

A math professor warned me of the dangers of an all-or-none life plan, and yet my grades continued to reflect my priorities. I left college midway through my junior year. Oddly, it was math that would have alerted me to reality.

On my own, out of school, and with only my golf game as a source of income, I took stock of the competition. By the time I'd added up all the college seniors who were turning pro, all the foreign players who had come here to live the dream, and all of the twenty-something, thirty-something, and forty-something journeyman pros who toiled on minitours around the country, I totaled some six thousand players who thought they just might be good enough to make a nice living at the game. And since only one hundred twenty-five players become exempt each year to play the PGA Tour, only two percent of those six thousand really make it.

I never made it anywhere near that two percent. However, like the milk offerings at your supermarket, professional golf offers its own skim version, whereby the fat—money—is drained off. These are the minitours, where players put up their own cash, usually five hundred dollars or so per tournament, and hope to finish in the top quarter of the field. Only those few players earn a livable wage. I rarely earned a livable wage. Mostly I packed my clubs in the trunk, drove hours to the next tournament site, and checked into yet another cheap hotel.

At this level the game nearly ate me alive. There was too much alone time, too many hours spent pondering my capacity to knock a ball into a hole with a stick. Moreover, the social network of college was absent, and I became just another young, unmarried player toiling in loneliness and obscurity.

The one piece of advice from my college coach that really stuck with me was this: "Chris, never allow the game *to define you* as a person. Never allow *any* occupation to define you."

I lived that minitour life for four years, until, at age twenty-five, I finally conceded to reality: Chris Hackett was never going to compete against the world's best, nor was he going to live in a big house in Arizona and drive a Ferrari. He would end up a golf range owner in Charleston, South Carolina, a college dropout making a modest living. He'd teach the proper swing to the after-work crowd, and perhaps, if God smiled, he'd meet "Mrs. Golfer."

As Cack and I continued to pace the grounds and note the yardages, those past strivings and failures jelled into experience, the kind that excited me and burst forth into a new priority. I wanted to find today's kids, today's Chris and J. T., and build into them the hope and courage to pursue their own dreams.

Frankly, I was tired of dealing with a largely adult clientele. That would have its place—Cack could handle the adults and insult them with gusto—but I wanted to feel very young again, to instruct pint-sized slicers and drink purple Kool-Aid and laugh at adolescent humor.

We had just finished rechecking the last measurement—I was recording it all in a notepad—when Cack suddenly ran some thirty yards along the back of the property. The height of the weeds prevented me from seeing anything below his shoulders.

"Cack . . .?" I called into my radio. "What's the matter?"

For a long moment there was silence. Then, "Boss man, we got a problem with this land."

"Can't be," I said. "It's ideal."

"Nope, we gotta problem."

"What now?"

"Gators. There's a swamp behind this property, and I see a nest of 'em just slitherin' in the muck. I can't be retrieving golf balls if there's gators and muck."

I thought through this problem quickly, much like the folks at Augusta National did when they discovered the pros could hit balls over their range fence and onto Washington Road. "After we get a fence up, we'll install an eighty-foot-tall net across the back of the range . . . no one will clear that."

I expected to hear him say, "Ten-four." Instead he paused a moment before blurting, "Mercy . . . he ate it."

I could not figure out why he said what he did. I pressed my talk button. "What'd you say, Cack?"

From across the weeds I saw him pointing with one hand, holding his walkie-talkie to his mouth with the other. "I left my Mountain Dew can back there on the bank, and a gator just ran up and ate the can."

"You'd better walk on back here to the road, Cackster."

He trudged back through the weeds and met me at the FOR LEASE sign. After fifteen minutes of weighing pros, cons, and what ifs, we agreed that this property qualified as one of our top three candidates, that indeed this land held strong possibilities.

Traffic was good here, sure, and the ground looked like it would support grass well—and Cack was raring to go, having already purchased a new high-powered bullhorn. But I could not commit yet, not until I searched the county to see if something even better had sprouted. I definitely wanted to avoid any land with a wooded area near where I'd locate the golf shop. Less timber meant less stuff could burn.

Though I was moving past my dance with disaster, my groundskeeper reminded me that such progress was not without scars.

Molly called late that night, just after I'd cleaned the red dirt off my shoes and tossed my soiled clothes into the washer.

"I've decided that twelve kids is a nice number," I said to her, intentionally vague.

Long, wary pause. "You would put a woman through…wait a sec, I'm adding this up. *One hundred and eight months* of pregnancy?!"

"No. Molly, I mean twelve kids per class. After-school and summer golf classes. That's the new thrust of my business."

"Oh." She sighed as if relieved. "Thank you for clearing that up."

She told me about her day—more mudslinging at a DC debate—and I updated her on the insurance settlement, which was okay but not great. I felt tired tonight, though, and wanted to discuss a serious topic before I offended her with frequent yawning. "Mol, I think we need to talk about the long distance thing."

"What about it? Are you now getting cold golfer feet, Chris Hackett?"

"No. We just need to talk. You see, I really love my job."

"All the time?"

"I love it most of the time. What about your own?"

"I love my job…sometimes."

"Most or some?"

"Somewhere between most and some."

"Okay, we'll call this a draw for now."

She laughed as if the subject intrigued her. "Isn't 'draw' a golf term that you once used in my lesson?"

"Yep, that's a shot that curves left. But then, I'm sure you have 'draws' in the political world."

"Especially after a debate, when the pundits can't decide who'll win, and then a news show takes a poll and it comes in fifty percent to fifty percent."

"If all else fails, at least we have that word in common."

"You're very chatty tonight."

"I'm in a better mood. Today Cack and I found a cool piece of land, and past the boundary fence is a wetlands. We might even conduct wildlife tours whenever he gets his new cart built."

"I'm glad you want to work with kids."

The last thing I told her before we ended our talk was that I wanted us both to pray about the pace with which we'd get to know one another. "I'll be glad to," she said.

We agreed that it was best to simply date when we could, talk frequently on the phone, and not rely on that easily misinterpreted beast, e-mail.

For the next three days, sunup to sundown, I searched other parcels of land. I walked flat country land in North Charleston, moist, marsh-front land on the Cooper River, tilled farm land much too far from the city to attract business, and a twenty-acre plot wedged between a park and a graveyard. This land I walked alone at midday, only my shadow to keep me company. Somewhere land and golf and entrepreneurship would meet and coagulate. And the more I thought about it, the more I liked the gator acreage.

I returned to that property the next day, noted the heavy traffic on the frontage road, the fast-food places just a quarter mile away, an elementary school a half mile past that. Somewhere in my head, coagulation occurred.

Once again, I stood in front of a huge real estate sign and dialed the phone number painted on its front, only this time the sign was By Owner. The lady owner wanted twenty-two hundred per month to lease her property, a reasonable sum—and she wasn't just any lady, certainly no stranger to either myself or to Cack. The owner of the land was Mrs. Dupree, who had purchased the property three years earlier, and for a far different purpose.

"My original plan was to raise dogs there, Chris," she explained over the phone. "Little one-brick dogs. Lots of them. But then I discovered—"

"That swamp full of gators?"

"The Department of Natural Resources said I couldn't remove them or shoot them, that they were protected. And you know how gators love a dog, especially little appetizer dogs."

"Yes, ma'am, I understand."

While I paced the edge of her property one more time, envisioning the next ten years of my life spent here—giving lessons, watching Cack insult the customers, possibly raising my own kids, and calling the Wildlife Department to come and remove yet another reptile from my driving range—I told Mrs. Dupree to draw up the lease papers, that I'd take it. Somehow I pictured having her as my landlord a far cry from Mr. Vignatti.

This new real estate, along with a thousand pounds of grass seed and nature's pledge of photosynthesis, was a very good thing.

27

LESSON FOR TODAY

Airline fares may seem expensive, but
they are a bargain compared to the
cost of loneliness.

Whatever it takes.

Those were my words, and they became more and more
applicable as the days rolled toward the elections. First I made
a day trip to DC. It was October 26, and Molly took me on a
tour of the aviation wing of the Smithsonian. This museum
was built as one enormous hangar not far from Dulles airport,
and it made for a great date. We even flirted beneath a 1935
crop duster:

"Would you have buzzed my farm in that thing if we'd
met in rural Kentucky in 1935?" she asked, loud enough to
embarrass a group of field-tripping junior high kids gathered
nearby.

"I'd have dusted the Cusack farm ten times a day," I replied,
also too loud.

She led me into the military section of the hangar, where I
noted the nose of an F-series fighter plane pointing at the nose
of a Russian MIG. We waited for the junior high kids to gather

again. "Molly," I asked, "if I had been a Russian pilot, would you have intercepted me in midair?"

She shook her head. "Not on the first date, but I'm sure our radars would have beeped in unison."

Behind us came giggles, whispers, and more giggles.

A half hour later we wandered into the space program exhibit. An entire Space Shuttle sat on display in there, as well as several Apollo-era capsules and space suits. By now we had lost the youth, and other than the museum's staff we had the exhibit all to ourselves.

Molly touched the glass of a capsule, which was smaller than I remembered from seeing them on TV. "Would you have bounded across moon craters to come visit me?" she asked, obviously not ready to end our silly banter.

"Hmmm. Low-gravity dating could be interesting, especially when traveling by foot."

And then, as we strolled out of the space program and made a right past the jetted history of Boeing, we found ourselves standing below something mammoth and silver. I had no idea that this was its resting place. Sixty-odd years after her day of infamy over Japan, the Enola Gay sat high above us, shiny and fully restored, perched there in all her glory.

Molly stared upward at the belly of the plane and whispered, "This one feels too important for flirtatious comments, Chris."

I moved beside her and craned my neck. "Agreed."

The sense of history was palpable; the plane renders one emotional simply from staring at it. It made me realize, in the same moment, both the consequences of defending freedom and the fragile nature of life. Molly seemed emotional as well, especially after I told her that my father, long deceased, had served in the Air Force. There are likely not many women who

have planted a kiss on their boyfriend in the shadow of the
Enola Gay, but Molly is one of them.

That night I accompanied her to a TV studio, where she was
to be interviewed on a cable show, this just two weeks before
elections. There sat Molly on a studio set, wearing the same flat-
tering blue outfit she'd worn in Charleston. She readied herself
between two cohosts, who alternately asked for her opinions on
the state's congressional battles, as well the nation as a whole.

Molly locked eyes with the camera. "The battles are as heated
as always," she said between very white teeth. "But an interesting phenomenon is occurring in New York: it's become popular
in some circles to try to trash opponents' outdoor pep rallies
by engaging in drive-by water balloonings."

"Did you say 'water ballooning'?" asked the cohost, serving
up a softball of a question.

Molly grinned once, nodded twice. "Yes. In fact, just last
week in the Bronx, I met a single man, a conservative who led a
group of water balloon tossers in throwing balloons at a large
gathering of protesting liberals. And this morning in Queens,
the liberals fired back, tossing blue water balloons at a campaign rally for the mayoral candidate. There in the Big Apple,
they're calling it 'water wars.'"

She had taken her act to New York, where apparently the politically minded citizens preferred balloons to golf balls. When Molly
departed the set after the interview, I took her by the hand and
told her that I was proud to be dating a professional pot stirrer.

Three weeks later she visited me in Charleston. She timed her
visit well—we caught a warm weekend in mid-November, and I

think I surprised her when I pulled up outside her hotel with the johnboat hitched to my truck. She knew it was an "outdoor" kind of date, though I had left out the particulars.

Something else I appreciated about her was how she refused to be a wait-on-the-dock-and-let-the-guy-do-everything kind of woman. At the launch ramp she helped push the boat off the trailer and never complained when her sneakers got wet. Then she jumped into my truck and parked it while I started the outboard engine.

Cape Romain's marshlands had faded along with most of the land foliage, and yet the low humidity seemed to energize the wildlife; some type of silvery fish kept jumping near the banks, and various shore birds rummaged for food along every sandbar we passed.

In the widest section of the inlet I set us to drift, and it was then that Molly turned from the front bench seat. We sat facing each other, only a small breeze rustling over the bow, just enough to unsettle the water.

"You like it out here, don't you?" she asked.

"It's peaceful. And the scenery is great…the brunette scenery, I mean."

She kept gazing at me, as if searching for something. Blank faced, she glanced at the sky for a moment, then back to me.

"What?" I asked, fighting the urge to hand her a paddle and ruin what felt like a serious moment.

She said, "I was just thinking about when we first met."

"Oh, when I almost scared you off?"

"You didn't scare me," she said, her voice unusually soft. "Not really. I'm glad you can talk freely about wanting to be a father."

At that I reached for the paddle and steered us into the next bend. "I'm glad that you're glad."

That was all we said for a long while. It seemed that we had reached the point in our relationship where bits of depth and seriousness freely intertwined with bouts of spontaneous fun. Around the bend, as she turned to look where we were headed, I spied a distant sandbar and decided that it was time for some of the latter.

"Molly?" She spun in her seat to face forward again.

"Yes?"

"Remember how, when I asked you last night what kind of outdoor activity you'd prefer today, you said, 'Maybe a walk, perhaps a game of putt-putt'?"

"I remember. But this little boat cruise was a great idea too."

I used the paddle to point to the tarp rolled up in the bow. "Well, ma'am, here at Hackett Outdoor Entertainment, we can do all of that."

She pulled the tarp out into the middle of the boat, and we unrolled it and pulled out the contents: two putters, four colored golf balls, five empty coffee cans, and a gardening spade.

Molly laughed and reached for the spade. "We're going to build our own course?"

"Without bulldozers or even any grass."

The sandbar we beached the boat upon was long and nearly oval in shape, and in less than twenty minutes we had constructed our course. Out in the estuaries, the sand gets packed hard by the weight of the water, and it makes for quite the smooth surface on which to putt. Trouble is, the advancing and receding tides allow a "course" to be open for only a few hours per day. I had always wanted to do this, no matter the temporal nature of it, and I felt elated that she greeted the idea with such enthusiasm.

We got a bit carried away building the last two holes—we made each of them more than two hundred feet in length and added a sand ramp that would launch a well-stuck ball over a pile of driftwood.

"It's like Evel Knievel golf," she said and swatted the first orange ball across damp sand.

I let her win the first match. But I did it with subtlety—such as on the third hole, when I hit my ball a bit too hard and watched it roll past the buried can and off the sandbar and down into the shallow waters.

"That's a penalty stroke, right?" she asked. Molly too had a certain competitive nature, one that served her well in her vocation.

After we had played the course several times, we noticed a gathering of spectators. They had either drifted in or flown in while we weren't looking. But now the pelicans and the gulls waddled up the far bank, eyeing our game as if they viewed our golf balls as rolling morsels, perhaps odd-shaped clams with a peculiar ability to rotate.

At a distance they followed us around the course until we arrived back at the boat. There Molly fed them the crust from a sandwich while I went and dug up the coffee cans and stowed them away in the tarp.

I was leaned over the johnboat with my back turned when she said with surprise, "Chris, they're so…fat!"

"Yep. Noticed that once before."

It was not the most earth-shattering date, nor was it over-the-top romantic. It was the kind of date where you realize how comfortable you are with the other person and how willingly each of you fits into the other's world.

Back at the boat ramp we fastened the straps from stern to trailer, and it was there that I asked her if she'd enjoyed herself.

"Coming after the election turmoil, you have no idea." She stuffed her life jacket under the bow and said, "This is so outside the Beltway. Not a single thing, not us, not the birds nor the jumping fish told a single lie about anyone else."

I pulled the drain plug and let the last bit of water run out the back of the boat. "Refreshing?"

"Very." She went around my truck, climbed into the passenger seat, and waited for me to scoot behind the steering wheel. "I'd really like to see the new site for your range. Especially since I sorta helped force the relocation."

Cack and I had already installed ten of the hitting mats, plus we'd erected the net on the far side of the range. Though the ground remained crude and uncarpeted with grass, and though we weren't even open for business yet, our younger clients didn't seem to care, particularly on a warm afternoon in November. When Molly and I arrived, Cack and six kids occupied the mats. They'd brought their own bags of used golf balls, and they all swatted away, balls flying high, low, and sideways.

I showed Molly the concrete foundation for the new shop—it had just been poured the previous day. Seconds later Cack spotted us, and we exchanged waves from across the construction site. I felt blessed to have his loyalty, as he could have so easily taken a full-time job elsewhere and left me without my most valuable employee.

Molly's third Carolina visit concluded just after we downloaded the same ring tone to our cell phones—the opening riff to an eighties song called "Burning Down the House."

It was her idea; she thought the song was funny and ironic. I acknowledged that it was at least ironic.

After I'd driven her to the airport and kissed her good-bye, I walked alone back across the lower level of a parking deck.

It was there in that cool shade where I replayed the ring tone and finally laughed out loud—partly because I accepted my fiery furnace for what it was and partly because I was sure I'd met the woman I would marry, but mostly because I realized yet again that God could engineer something good out of what originally seemed disastrous.

EPILOGUE

"Aim at that tree," I said to the Darwinist.

He was a middle-aged golf beginner, a first-timer to my new range, and for twenty minutes he'd rejected my fundamental instructions on proper grip, stance, and alignment. Only now, after I'd presented him with clear evidence that I knew what I was talking about, did he start to cave.

"Which tree?" he replied, his grip and stance evolving into something resembling a golfer's.

I pointed beyond the net at the end of my range, to a cypress that grew angled from the swamp. "The tree that the squirrel just ran up."

He squinted. "You mean the squirrel that formed from an amoeba four billion centuries ago?"

"Yes, that very squirrel."

He addressed each ball with scientific precision and attempted three shots. *Duff. Shank. Whiff.*

"I'm terrible at this!" he complained and plunged his 8-iron back into his golf bag.

Out of nowhere Cack zoomed past us in his cart. "Just give it a few million years, dude!" he shouted through the bullhorn, loud enough to stir every hacker on my range. "By then golf will be extinct, and you'll have the perfect excuse not to play the game."

The guy had no sense of humor, however, and after five more frustrating minutes he told me he'd either figure it out for himself or take Cack's advice and quit.

In much better moods at Hack's Grand Opening were my longtime friends and clients, lined up on the hitting mats, swatting away, and begging to be insulted. There was Officer Cavin, hacking away next to Benny, who hacked away next to Mrs. Dupree, followed by Pauly Three Seeds, Mr. Roycroft, Tongue Depressuh, Jerry Schooler, Lin Givens, the Bubbas, the conservative teenagers who did not dress conservatively, and my most attractive client, Molly, who had flown down for the event. Past the adults, some four dozen kids fired away, all trying to wallop the loudmouth.

Behind the mats stood a small wooden sign that read This Way to Misery Hill→. That was Cack's term for the golf range, and the window in my new shop offered a grand view of it all. It wasn't just any window, either. In keeping with Charleston's coastal geography, my builder had installed a huge glassed porthole, some five feet in diameter, from which I could observe all the misery taking place on misery hill. And on this fifth day of March, the misery quotient ran high. Even without the eighty-foot-high netting at the end of the range, the reptiles cruising the swamp knew they were in little danger of getting hit.

Bullhorn raised, Cack zeroed in on my girlfriend and made sure everyone could hear him. "Oh, look at Miss Politics on mat number nine! She's so busy making goo-goo eyes at Chris, she whiffed the ball!" Molly blushed, then sought refuge with the teenagers and joined them in throwing handfuls of balls at Cack.

He circled around the 100-yard marker and accelerated toward Pauly. "Pauly *Three Seeds*? What kind of a name is

THAT?! Maybe he lives off bird seed....He must, since his golf swing is so weak, he couldn't break an egg."

Pauly too turned red and struck ball after ball, all of them flying wide of target.

Cack, however, remained a bit wary of Lin. On his next pass she buzzed a shot right past his windshield. He raised the bullhorn again. "That's the way to hit like a...like a...woman who practices a lot."

In the golf shop I thanked each friend and stranger who had come out. I also asked them—if they felt so inclined—to contribute a sentence to a new journal displayed on the counter for all to flip through and read. Everyone who contributed had to begin their sentence with the same phrase: *Golf is hard because . . .*

The first page held four entries and portrayed well the diversity of opinion on the subject:

Golf is hard because they put the hole too far away, plus you don't get any do-overs.

Golf is hard because it is unnatural, unlike childbirth, which seems to come so naturally for me that I now have six rug rats and a seventh on the way.

Golf is hard because actually striking the ball and making it go where you want is ten times harder than it looks when you watch the pros on TV, and you just know those pros were all born at swanky country clubs and didn't ever have to do chores like mow the grass or clean their rooms, they probably had maids do it all and so they spent their entire youth on a golf course and this is why golf is hard for anyone who wasn't born to rich parents and did not win the gene pool of life.

Golf is hard because it's impossible! It's like trying to swat a gnat from the air with a chopstick, only worse.

Though today was the official grand opening, Hack's had been open for weeks. I'd waited until we had a better chance of

warm weather, and March did not disappoint. After much discussion with my groundskeeper, I'd also decided to concentrate
a full sixty percent of the business on kids—elementary, high
school, junior high, kindergarten, the entire circus train of
youth. We contacted every school within a thirty mile radius,
offering afternoon programs twice a week, plus discounts,
whatever it took.

Parents gushed that two hundred golf balls for six bucks
was very cheap babysitting—and Cack, well, he knew how to
make the experience fun.

He'd already cut from full sheets of plywood a Tyrannosaurus Rex, a Darth Vader, and a King Kong, then painted
them green, black, and dark brown, respectively, all with gri-
maces on their faces. These he stood upright out on the left
side of the range, propped from behind with two-by-fours and
spaced at distances of thirty, fifty, and seventy-five yards. Give
them a target, an Astroturf hitting mat, and a large supply of
golf balls, and kids will stay out there forever.

Cack's new customized cart was the bigger rage: In keeping
with our new location and the creatures that lived beyond the
fence, he'd fashioned a huge smiling gator face to the front.
The protective cage still resembled a top hat, and this gave the
gator a kind of formal appearance, as if it would rather munch
you in tux and tails.

The kids, of course, ate this up, especially when my groundskeeper employed his bullhorn: "All right, you kiddie hackers,
if you can't whack the Cack, you don't earn your snack!"

And he meant it. He would not give those children a
drink unless they could hit his cart with a ball. It was a new
form of motivation, and it did wonders for the kids' abilities, not to mention their concentration. The more talented
and hardworking kids would sometimes hit Cack at fifty or

a hundred yards away…but then he would circle closer and closer, sometimes to just ten feet away, until every last child had hit the cart.

We also used his cart for Saturday morning wildlife tours, cramming five or six youngsters inside with us and paralleling the swamp at the far end of the range, only a chain-link fence and our net to separate man from beast. On the way out across the grass, Cack built up a bit of fear in the kids by assuming the voice and comportment of a tour operator: "To your right you'll notice the gigantic turtle known as an alligator snapper, with jaws strong enough to crush a golf ball or bite the tires off your mommy's minivan."

Invariably, the youngsters reacted as one, "Whoooa."

I often wondered if Cack and I would make more money if we just went ahead and declared ourselves a day care.

Parents picked up their kids at the front door and were greeted with lines that cracked me up. When asked by a mother or father, "Did you have fun?" the kids answered with lines like, "Yeah, I hit the loudmouth man with a ball and almost got to pet a crocodile."

The appeal of running a kid-centric business rather than an adult-centric one affected me in a surprising way. I no longer obsessed over money but instead concentrated on what I did best—teaching and encouraging the students. The income was steady and consistent, perhaps a slight upslope on the graph of revenue.

More important to me, these kids had no self-serving agendas other than to enjoy themselves, to hang out with other kids, and to gain proficiency in the sport. They just hit ball after ball, frowning at the bad shots and celebrating the good. Hour after hour they fired at the targets, thrusting little fists in the air and whooping out loud whenever they hit one. Sometimes a ball would hit a spot on the painted plywood where the paint was not quite dry, and this left a visible mark. Kong himself grew polka-dotted.

We even had kid-sized plastic chairs set out behind the mats to host the inevitable breaks for jungle juice and gummy bears. Cack told a gathering of youngsters that gummy bears were the most nonnutritious food since those orangy circus peanuts, this from a man whose chief dietary supplement was a six-pack of Mountain Dew.

That evening, just before sunset and after most of the crowd had departed, Molly burst through the door and pointed back over her shoulder to the range. "Chris, you gotta see this. There's a kid out there in dirty sneakers who is incredible … maybe even better than you!"

I looked up from reading the latest journal entries. "Who? Show me."

She grabbed my hand, and I followed her out the door. At the far end of the range I saw the kid by himself, a pile of balls beside him. Molly said, "He's already knocked two teeth out of Tyrannosaurus Rex and clanged three balls off the side of Cack's cart."

We had a long walk to reach him, and en route I watched him fire away, one ball after another, all of them landing in a tight dispersion around the 150-yard marker. He looked perhaps ten or eleven, of slender build and olive skin.

I wandered over, offered the kid a wink, and introduced myself.

He shook my hand and told me his name was Camilo and that he was indeed eleven.

I stood behind him, watched him smash two more shots. "How did you get started in the game, Camilo?" I asked.

Soft-spoken and a bit shy, he kept his gaze on the ground. "I used to hit balls into an old fishing net in my backyard, but I like it here better because I can see if the balls curve in the air or go straight."

Despite his shyness, he was as articulate in conversation as he was skilled with a golf club.

"Has your dad or your mom helped you learn?" I inquired next, holding his golf bag upright and checking out his equipment—which was decent but in need of new grips.

He only shook his head.

"No one has instructed you?" I feigned shock at how any kid could hit a ball so precisely.

He teed another ball and took a practice swing. "I just like to practice."

I pulled his 7-iron from his bag and handed it to him and asked him to hit a ball at Kong and make it curve left. This he did without comment. Molly's mouth fell agape. I rolled another ball onto the grass near his feet and asked him to make this one start out at Darth Vader and then curve right. This too he did without hesitation. The kid was talent incarnate. Molly stood speechless.

"How did you learn to do that?" I asked him. "You're at least four levels ahead of everyone else. Maybe five levels."

Camilo shrugged and used his club to roll another ball in front of him. He adjusted his stance and said, "Well, I watch the pros on TV a lot, but what helps me most is five years of hitting at moving targets."

Molly cocked her head to me and said, "*Moving* targets?"

Camilo burst into a grin, as if he could not hold our secret any longer. "We're just teasing you, ma'am," he said. "Chris has been my instructor ever since I was six years old. I was his first student."

Her playful slap to my shoulder was just what I deserved.

Camilo exchanged a high five with me and returned to his practice session. He was my most dedicated junior player. Over the years he and I had pulled our little stunt at least a half dozen times.

After everyone had left, after the lights were turned off and we'd bid Cack good night, Molly and I strolled out onto the darkened range and sat in two of the plastic kiddie chairs, our feet tapping at random moments. The night felt cool and crisp, not yet hinting at spring. My plan for weeks had been to propose to Molly on Easter weekend. But now I felt that was too far off, that I didn't want to wait much longer, perhaps not past tomorrow night, when we'd booked a dinner cruise out of a local marina.

I always enjoyed surprising her. And, as it turned out, she held a similar affection. At some hour short of midnight, we both had our heads tilted back, perusing the stars over Charleston, when she nudged my foot. "Hey."

"Hey."

"I have some news. Some good news."

"Tell me."

"I've been offered a position with a Charleston TV station. It's equal in pay, but with more vacation time."

Now it was my turn to be speechless.

She nudged my foot a second time. "Since we've talked so often recently of our relationship moving toward permanence, I just thought I'd get a head start."

I sat up in my kiddie chair but still could not form words.

"Go ahead, Chris," she encouraged, "say what you're thinking of saying. I want you to."

"But...of course I *want* to, it's just that—"

"Go ahead, say those little words. I need to hear you say it."

I gulped night air and exhaled slowly. "But, but how'd you know?"

"I saw it in your eyes today, when our eyes locked from across your range. I want to hear it."

"You really think it's time?"

"Say it. I want to hear you say it."

"Okay…Good golly, Miss Molly!"

AUTHOR'S NOTE

A golf range is not called "misery hill" for nothing. In all of golf, there is perhaps no activity that induces more misery in the participant than beginners sweating on some range, trying their best to fix their golf swings, doing their best to strike with power and accuracy a white ball that sits motionless on green grass. *It looks so easy.*

My own time on misery hill grew far less frustrating when, at the age of fifteen, my family moved west and I met a top junior golfer in Texarkana, Texas. We were the same age, and we introduced ourselves beside a pond bisecting the third hole of Northridge Country Club—where we both had the same idea of using a summer afternoon to dive into the pond to collect free golf balls. Throughout high school and into our college years, we practiced together and competed in tournaments, until I moved back across the country to South Carolina. My friend is Geoff Jones, owner and operator of the Texarkana Golf Learning Center, father of two, husband of one, and an expert at teaching the intricacies of the golf swing. His clients include junior champions, professionals, and several NCAA All-Americans. This book is dedicated to Geoff, and to our fellow members of the Texas High Golf Team.

Those were the days....

READING GROUP GUIDE

CHRIS'S QUESTIONS:

1. In the midst of my initial crush on Molly, I did and said things that were out of character, just to impress her. Whom do you know who has acted out of character when in the midst of a crush? Did the crush turn into "twu wuv"? Engagement? "Mawage"?

2. President Bush has become quite a controversial public figure. How did you feel about Dubya stopping by my driving range? Also, if a President shanks a golf ball and it breaks a spectator's bifocals, is the ball then deemed a weapon of glass destruction?

3. After my business was destroyed, I had to get away one afternoon, be by myself. So I paddled my johnboat into a saltwater estuary, where I felt alone with nature and with God. Do you have a special place you go when life throws up a stumbling block? Do you view God as being everywhere in your surroundings, or do you view him as a kind of invisible man, of average height and weight, who only shows up when you are alone in your special place?

MOLLY'S QUESTIONS:

1. As a political correspondent, I found that many people stereotyped me as a hard-charging, climb-the-corporate-ladder female. Now I find that many of my friends were shocked that I would leave the political environment to work closer to Chris. Have you ever left a vocational pursuit to pursue love? "Twu wuv," or just "puppy wuv"?

2. Would you take up golf if you really liked a guy?

3. Do you have all of the U.S. presidents memorized? Why not?

4. Do you think any of Calvin Coolidge's staff called him "Coolio"?

CACK'S QUESTIONS:

1. Driving ranges are a study in human behavior—each person alone with his or her bucket of golf balls, with little or no interaction with anyone else. Do you think driving ranges would be livelier and more fun if someone drove around the range in a golf cart and insulted the customers through a bullhorn? Would you man the bullhorn? Who would you like to insult?

2. Have you ever gone on a date to a driving range?

3. Do you consider Mountain Dew a health drink?

PAULY THREE SEEDS'S QUESTIONS:

1. Most people think accountants are boring number-crunchers, with little personality. The majority of my friends think that I am a boring number-cruncher, with little personality. But sometimes late at night, in the quiet of my kitchen, I moonwalk across the linoleum. What do you do for fun when no one is looking?

2. Will there be any boring people in heaven? Will those that get there have to walk around like conformist robots, or will there be jumping and dancing and running just for the fun of it?

3. If I were to write a book on what heaven might be like, would a good title be *Moonwalking on Streets of Gold*?

4. How does one *get* to heaven?

GLOSSARY

Blue tees: The back tees, sometimes referred to as the "men's tees," which is a totally sexist concept and also degrades any woman who can really play the game.
Contributed by Lin Givens, 3-handicapper currently residing in San Francisco.

Bogey: When a single male golf instructor allows a potential date to think he gambles with his students.
Contributed by Chris Hackett, scratch golfer currently residing in Charleston.

Double bogey: Jumping to conclusions when your single male golf instructor tells you he made a wager with a woman.
Contributed by Molly Cusack, terrible golfer currently residing in Charleston.

Fader: A date who eats too much and falls asleep in the movie theatre. Also, a golfer whose shots curve slightly to the right.
Contributed by Benny's wife, a golf beginner currently residing in Charleston.

First tee: In golf, the manicured turf on which a person strikes their first shot. In dating, the softly lit restaurant where dim lights hide the wrinkles and gray hairs of the person with whom you've been set up.
Contributed by Mrs. Dupree, currently raising a litter of long-haired brickettes in a swanky suburb of Charleston.

Golf attire: For seniors—gaudy plaids and lots of polyester. For the younger, country club set—basic khaki pants and pastel all-cotton shirts. For hip-hop dudes—baggy jeans, NFL jerseys, and caps turned sideways. Oh, and a bit of jewelry, if one can afford it.

Contributed by Tongue Depressuh, 14-handicapper currently residing in a dorm room at the University of Florida.

Hazard: Usually a pond or creek, sometimes surrounded by lush flora and breathtaking shrubbery. Also, allowing your daughter to date a guy with no job, little education, and no future.

Contributed by Mr. Roycroft, nursery owner and non-golfer, currently residing in Florence, SC.

Penalty stroke: What anyone deserves who thinks that a one-sentence questionnaire asking who was the fifteenth President of the United States will help solve an arson case.

Contributed by Jonathan, arson investigator and newfound golf nut, currently residing in Charleston.

Range hound: Someone who spends excessive amounts of time at the local driving range. Not to be confused with a bar hound, which is a guy who spends excessive amounts of time in various bars, hoping to meet the right woman; or a singles group hound, which is a guy who spends excessive amounts of time in various church singles groups, also hoping to meet the right woman.

Contributed by Jay Jarvis, 17-handicapper, currently residing in Ecuador.

Red tees: The forward tees, where juniors can shoot lower scores on a shorter course and thus think they are better than they actually are.

Contributed by the conservative teenagers who do not dress conservatively.

Scorecard: For a female, this is where she journals the events and happenings within a relationship. For a male, this is a card of eighteen little squares in which he pencils in his golf scores.

Contributed by Darcy, one half of the worst husband/wife golf team in history, currently residing in Greenville, SC.

Tee time: That afternoon hour when British citizens who flunked spelling sit in their parlors and sip their favorite beverage.

Contributed by the Darwinist dude, 36-handicapper who hails from London.

Trajectory: For women, the forward momentum of a relationship. For men, the forward momentum of a golf shot.

Contributed by Cack Pruitt, groundskeeper and master of the bullhorn, currently residing in Charleston.

Triple bogey: Thinking that hosting political rallies at a golf range is a great idea.

Contributed by Chris, Molly, and Cack.

Yardage markers: Occasions that mark significant forward momentum in a relationship, such as flowers in the first month, a necklace in the third, and an engagement ring in the sixth.

Contributed by Pauly Three Seeds, 8-handicapper currently residing in Mt. Pleasant, SC.

CREDITS

Lin Fore gave me a very informative tour of the Cape Romain National Wildlife Refuge. Lin guides in the coastal waters of South Carolina and has entertained my group of friends on several saltwater fishing expeditions.

Joseph "Joey" Schooler, longtime friend and Charlestonian golf buddy, provided info. on insurance details.

Various golf buddies encouraged me to write this story, including Ted, Charles, Jonathan, Josh, Jackson, Bruce, Joey, Tony, Sandy, Kati, Patrick, Mike H., Todd, Mike C., Senter, Geoff, and Matt K., who usually whiffs the ball because he prefers fishing and playing the guitar.

ABOUT THE AUTHOR

Ray Blackston lives and writes in South Carolina. He left the corporate world in 2000 to focus on creative writing. In 2003, his first novel, *Flabbergasted*, was one of three finalists for the Christy Award for best first novel, and was chosen as Inspirational Novel of the Year by the *Dallas Morning News*. More of Ray's background is available at his Web site, www.rayblackston.com.

If you liked *Par for the Course* . . .

A PAGAN'S
NIGHTMARE

A tongue-in-cheek look at contemporary culture through the eyes of a screenwriter who pens a hit about the last unbeliever on earth navigating a thoroughly Christian world.

An unwary "pagan" discovers he's one of the last remaining unbelievers in a world populated by Christians. Or so imagines Larry Hutch, a copywriter with hopes of writing a hit screenplay. While struggling in his faith and dealing with personal crises, he imagines a strange new world where song lyrics are altered to conform to "Christian" standards (the Beatles belt out "I Wanna Hold Your Tithe") and French fries, newly labeled "McScriptures," are tools for evangelism. Larry's screenplay is a big hit with his agent, Ned, but Ned's Southern Baptist wife is less than amused. Both men's futures will be on the line when the world witnesses A PAGAN'S NIGHTMARE.

Available now at a bookstore near you!